"Let g[o] of m[e]"

Ruth panicked. Blake's kiss had been too fast, too intense—too good.

"Ruth, I want you!" With a groan he pulled her back into his arms and kissed her without restraint. "Don't you know what you're doing to me?"

"I don't want to hear that!" She wrenched away from him.

"Ruth, we've worked together every day for months and we were attracted from the start. Why deny it?"

She couldn't look at him now. It was the truth. Yes, she wanted him. But Blake was absolutely the wrong man for her to get involved with. She looked at him helplessly. "I'm not the type who indulges in casual sex," she said. "It's not my style."

"*Casual?* You and me casual?" Suddenly he was angry. "I know what ails you. You're still in love with Garry, but you want me physically."

Ruth shot to her feet. He was wrong about Garry. But she certainly couldn't tell him the truth—that it was he she loved. Love wasn't part of what Blake had in mind.

CLAUDIA JAMESON lives in Berkshire, England, with her husband and family. She is an extremely popular author in both the Harlequin Presents and Harlequin Romance series. And no wonder! Her lively dialogue and ingenious plots—with the occasional dash of suspense—make her a favorite with romance readers everywhere.

Books by Claudia Jameson

HARLEQUIN PRESENTS

HARLEQUIN ROMANCE

These books may be available at your local bookseller.

Don't miss any of our special offers. Write to us at the following address for information on our newest releases.

Harlequin Reader Service
901 Fuhrmann Blvd., P.O. Box 1397, Buffalo, NY 14240
Canadian address: P.O. Box 603,
Fort Erie, Ont. L2A 9Z9

CLAUDIA JAMESON

one dream only

Harlequin Books

TORONTO • NEW YORK • LONDON
AMSTERDAM • PARIS • SYDNEY • HAMBURG
STOCKHOLM • ATHENS • TOKYO • MILAN

Harlequin Presents first edition October 1986
ISBN 0-373-10922-9

Original hardcover edition published in 1985
by Mills & Boon Limited

CHAPTER ONE

THE post always came a little later on Saturdays. Ruth Boyd was waiting eagerly for a letter from Saudi Arabia, from her fiancé, she was longing to know his reaction to the news of her winning such a large sum of money. She was longing most especially to know what he thought of the pamphlets she'd sent him, the details of the new houses being built just a few miles outside the city. Oh, they were ideal, those neat, two-bedroom homes, perfect for a newly-wed couple!

But at eight o'clock on that particular Saturday morning, about an hour before the post was due, Garry's eagerly awaited letter was actually the last thing on her mind. For the moment she had forgotten it, she had forgotten him, she could think of nothing but the phone call she had just received about her sister-in-law.

Ruth sat by the window in the living-room of the terraced house where she lived with her parents, letting her tears flow freely as she stared unseeingly at the small back garden. Poor Wendy, *poor* Wendy! Yet again she had lost the baby she had been carrying, the baby she so desperately wanted and, this time, her pregnancy had lasted almost five months. How awful, how *awful* it must be to miscarry after such a long time! How awful to miscarry at all . . . and this was the third time it had happened.

Closing her eyes against tears which just kept flowing, Ruth cringed inwardly at the memory of her brother's voice. He had sounded so wretched over the phone, so—so helpless. She could well imagine the emotions which had been churning behind that toneless, lifeless voice. Derek wanted a family of his own every bit as much as his wife did and—well, everyone had thought it would be all right this time, that Wendy would go full term and have that which she wanted more than anything in the world, a child of her own.

'But—but what *happened*?' On hearing Derek's news, Ruth had clutched the back of a chair for support, feeling crushed with disappointment. The call had come at seven-thirty that morning, just as she was padding her way to the kitchen to make her first tea of the day. Derek had phoned from the hospital, he had been there all night, he said, waiting, hoping the baby might be saved . . . 'When did it start? Oh, Derek, I'm so sorry!'

She had listened, biting hard on her lip as her brother explained that Wendy had simply started bleeding the previous night, as she and Derek were on their way to bed. 'There's no rhyme or reason to it, Ruth. I don't know why it happened' . . . Yes, she has. I promise you, Wendy had rested and done everything the doctors told her to. I've just had a long talk with one of them now and he—all of them—they're as much at a loss as I am.' He'd added this with a hint of bitterness which was totally out of character. 'If the doctors can't explain it, how can I? I mean, there's no apparent reason for her miscarrying. Wendy's healthy, strong, young . . .'

And heartbroken. That had been Derek's answer when Ruth had asked him how Wendy was feeling now, how she had taken it. Right now she was sleeping, having been sedated. That she was heartbroken went without saying.

Moaning softly, Ruth leaned forward as she sat, wrapping her arms tightly around her overweight cat as it leapt on to her knee and nuzzled against her. 'Oh, Tabatha! Why do such awful things have to happen? And why should it happen to Wendy when she's such a sweet, generous girl?'

Not a sound came from the cat, she merely wriggled in protest against the way she was being held so tightly. A great shuddering sob escaped from Ruth and fresh tears poured down her cheeks. The tears were for Wendy, for Derek, for their disappointment. She was hurting every bit as much as they were. Sometimes she wished she were not so soft, so sensitive, sometimes she got impatient with herself because of this. She was one of those people who couldn't even bear to watch the news because it hurt so often, because she got very easily upset by the atrocities that went on in the world. But this one had not been caused by mankind itself, the hurt she felt now was not the result of one person inflicting misery upon another. This was . . . Fate? One of those things that are sent to try us? All she wanted to do right now was to go to her sister-in-law, put her arms around her and say encouraging, comforting things to her. But that would have to wait until Tuesday, she had next week off work and had planned to visit Derek and Wendy for a few days in any case, but she couldn't go before Tuesday because on Monday she had a driving test, tomorrow she had a double driving lesson and this afternoon she had to go shopping for the old lady next door.

No, going to Essex today was impossible, unfortunately. She loved Wendy as much as she loved her brother and she missed them both terribly. They lived just outside Dagenham, where they had moved eighteen months earlier when Derek had been promoted within the finance company he worked for. He worked in the City of London now, at the firm's

Head Office, and his removal from Wolverhampton to the south had been something he welcomed while the rest of the family had lamented it.

The rest of the family? Oh, but they were all so scattered these days! Her other sibling, Helen, was living in Australia with her husband, her three-year-old daughter and the baby girl she had given birth to just three weeks ago. Another niece Ruth would not see for . . . heaven knew how long. If ever.

It was for this reason that her parents had gone to Australia to visit. They had been staying with Helen for the past five weeks and were not due back for another three. Helen had married when she was Ruth's age, twenty-two (Ruth had just turned twenty-two), and had moved to Australia within a year. She was now twenty-five and was dearly missed in spite of the letters, slides and cassettes which were very frequently exchanged.

Still, at least her parents had been able to make the journey. Norma and Reginald Boyd had been determined to do that as soon as Reg retired, which he had some months ago, at sixty. Norma was the same age and had also retired from her job at sixty, having worked since Ruth had left school. And now they were in Australia, at Helen's house in Queensland, enjoying their long-awaited, two-month visit with their first daughter.

It was Ruth's turn next. Her turn to leave home, that is. Her turn, her time, to marry. She and Garry had long since set the date. She and Garry had planned their lives very carefully. Theirs was to be a November wedding.

Ruth's fiancé was a nurse, a dedicated one, but he had felt no compunction in leaving England to work in Saudia Arabia for financial reasons. He was nursing there, working in a large, ultra-modern hospital. He had been talking of doing this when she had first met him in the Building Society where she worked. He had come in to open an account at the branch at which Ruth was secretary to the Manager, was saving for his own home, as indeed they both were now. For *their* home!

As her thoughts shifted on to happier ground, Ruth's tears subsided a little. She made a conscious effort to stop them altogether, smiling inwardly because it was this very sensitivity which Garry admired in her. He never minded when she cried easily, when she got upset on other people's behalf, even strangers. He called her his 'tender love' and said she must never change or even try to. He loved her just as she was.

At the unmistakable sound of something being pushed into the letter box, Ruth dropped Tabatha gently to her feet and went quickly into the hall, only to be disappointed as she saw it was the morning paper that had arrived. Only then did she wonder whether Garry had received her last letter to him. This had never occurred to her before. Surely he had? He had never failed to get any of her letters in all the time he'd been away, five months in all. And always, except for the last time, his reply had come by return of post. Of course that took days, but still. He had always written on the day he got her letter. She did not give up. After all, the post hadn't been delivered yet.

Instead she went into the kitchen, put the kettle on and splashed cold water on to her eyes while waiting for it to boil. She felt incredibly sad, curiously dazed, her mind was now working busily with a mixture of thoughts and emotions ... thinking of Derek and Wendy and their loss ... and her sister Helen and her new baby ... her parents' telephone call to her when they'd announced the news ...

Maybe she could try to get a call through to Garry at the hospital in Saudi?

It was odd, *odd*, that she hadn't heard from him yet. This, when in her last letter she had told him the incredible news that she had won five thousand pounds on the Premium Bonds! She had had a block of one hundred Premium Bonds since her nineteenth birthday and had never won a bean—until now! Two weeks ago she had won *five thousand pounds*! She couldn't wait for Garry's reaction to the news. Already the money was in the Building Society and had added very substantially to their savings. Not only could they afford a hefty deposit on a new house now, they could also afford to furnish one! Why, if they had known this would happen, Garry needn't have gone to work abroad in the first place! Would he come back prematurely, now they had achieved much more than the sum they had been saving for? Or would he stay for the full year, keep sending the money as he had so far? Would he have a choice about staying? He had committed himself to stay for a full year, would he be held to that commitment?

But Garry Anderson was not coming back at all. At least, he wasn't coming back to Ruth. She learned this within two minutes of the post being delivered. At the instant it dropped from the letter box, she was pouring boiling water into the teapot and though she couldn't see the front door from the kitchen, she just knew Garry's letter had arrived.

And there it was, in a blue airmail envelope with zigzag markings and stamps which no longer looked strange to her, nestling between several other envelopes, all of which were addressed to her father and were probably bills. She plucked Garry's letter from the pile, her pot of tea forgotten, and settled in an armchair to read it. The envelope contained only a single, lightweight sheet written in Garry's precise, fine hand, and even when she'd read the contents twice, she could neither understand nor believe what his words told her.

He had met someone else, the words said. He had fallen in love in a way he had never dreamed possible, the words said. With another nurse, a girl called Angela. He was sorry, he said, desperately so. Could she ever forgive him? Could she ever understand? Could she, as he urged her to, believe that nobody was more surprised at this event than he?

Could she? Ruth could do none of these things. Dazed, disbelieving, she read the letter over and over and over again. She was still looking for a mention of her last letter to him, still expecting to read what she had expected his letter to say, still scanning the lines for his enthusiastic reaction to her winnings, his enthusiastic reaction to the details of the house she wanted to put a deposit on. She simply could not take in what her fiancé was telling her. It was a long time before she realised she had received what her father would call a 'Dear John' letter.

It was a long time before she realised that the telephone was ringing, too. When the noise finally penetrated her trance-like state, she looked at the instrument as though it were an alien thing which didn't belong in her world. By the small telephone table, Tabatha sat, looking at her with that intense curiosity peculiar to cats.

Even then, blinking her way back to reality as she was, it was not the phone but her pet's 'Meoww!' that brought Ruth to her feet. She got up slowly, feeling so disorientated she had to hold on to the furniture as she made her way to the shrilling telephone. 'All right, Tabby, all right, I'm coming.' Wordlessly she put the receiver to her ear.

It was Mrs Edwards, the old lady who had lived next to her parents for more years than Ruth had lived. She knew it was Mrs Edwards, somewhere in her brain, yet she heard herself asking, 'Who is it?'

'It's me, love.' The old lady sounded puzzled, then concerned. 'Are you all right, Ruth? You sound very strange.'

'Y-yes, I . . .' I've just been jilted, she wanted to say. I've just been jilted but I am all right. Yet—yet I also feel ill, *ill*. Oh, Mrs Edwards, what am I going to do now? '. . . I—I've just woken up, that's all. Sorry about that.' She forced herself to finish the sentence, to laugh. The sound came out jerkily and, unwell though she was, the old lady sensed that something was amiss.

'Just woken up? But you're always up early, even when you're not working! What is it, love? I mean, it's turned ten o'clock!'

Was it really? Ruth glanced down at her wrist, only to realise that she wasn't dressed yet, let alone wearing her watch. Where had the past two hours gone? She had been awake since seven-thirty, since Derek's phone call . . .

She kept her conversation with her neighbour brief and polite. Mrs Edwards had always been Mrs Edwards to Ruth; that's how things were. Though she had been in Ruth's life all of Ruth's life, the younger woman would never presume to call her Maude, it just wasn't done, somehow.

When the call was finished Ruth's eyes came to rest on those of her aptly named tabby cat. 'Don't look at me like that, darling Tabby. I feel just as bemused as you look right now. It can't be true, can it? It must be a flash in the pan. Maybe it's a joke, a sick joke. Garry's in love with *me*, I know he is! Things like this don't happen in real life. Do they?'

Tabatha followed her into the kitchen, leapt on to a stool and watched as she made tea, this time with a solitary tea bag in a mug. She had to keep going. She had things to do. She had to do Mrs Edwards' shopping. She had to go in to town. What was it her neighbour had just said? What was it she wanted adding to her modest little shopping list? Tea? Coffee? No, no, it wouldn't be coffee, Mrs Edwards never touched the stuff. But it was one of the basics . . . now what *was* it?

Ruth's thinking was no clearer by the time she got into town. She managed that task simply because she went into town every day, to work, and often on her Saturdays off. She worked every third Saturday. It was simply a question of treading the familiar path to the bus-stop, getting on the bus when it deigned to come along, getting off and heading left towards the department store instead of right towards the Building Society. She didn't notice it was raining, didn't even notice that the early March winds were driving the heavy downpour against her face, drenching her uncovered head.

She had pulled on her gaberdine before leaving the house but she hadn't thought to pick up her brolly. Nor had she had the presence of mind to put on a rain hat. As it was she was soaked, her long black hair clinging limply against smooth, unnaturally white cheeks. Her soft, chocolate-brown eyes were like saucers, round, unseeing, unfocused. They were her most attractive feature, but today they looked too large for her face, contrasting starkly with her ghostly pale skin. A tall, slim figure trudging slowly through the rain, she looked exactly like what she was, a girl in a daze, a girl who'd had two awful shocks within the space of two awful hours. Not that she realised how she looked.

Nor did she realise she was crossing the busy road against the traffic lights. She didn't even blink when the horn of a car only inches from her blared deafeningly. As if coming from a long way off, she heard the noise, heard the screech of brakes, the hiss of rubber against a wet surface.

She simply walked on.

There was the slam of a car door, there was a deep, masculine voice shouting something about a stupid woman. Still she didn't realise it was she who was being referred to, that she had almost got herself killed. It was only when a large, long-fingered hand closed painfully around her wrist and yanked her around so violently she almost lost balance that Ruth was made aware of exactly what she was doing and where she was.

She was standing smack in the middle of the busiest shopping street in Wolverhampton. The lights had changed, people were milling around her, brushing against her as they crossed the road, having to deviate from a straight line because of the red car parked halfway across the junction. And the man who had hold of her, who was glaring down at her from a very superior height, was presumably its driver.

He didn't speak to Ruth so much as blast her with his fury, his words coming as rapidly as bullets from a machine-gun, yet failing nevertheless to penetrate the fog in her mind. 'What the hell do you think you're doing? Are you on a suicide mission or something?'

'Sorry,' she muttered, knowing she had done something wrong but unsure and uncaring quite what it was.

The man did not release her, rather his grip tightened, making her flinch involuntarily. She stared up at him, at a loss to understand him, and found herself looking into eyes so clear, so blue, so angry they were almost sparking. Apart from the eyes she had only an impression of very black hair, very lean features and what she would call a mean mouth if she were thinking normally. 'Listen, lady, if you choose to walk around like a zombie, that's your business, but I'd suggest you do it somewhere other than the town centre. There are other people roaming this earth, you know, and some of them are driving cars. I'm one of those people, and that,' he hissed, jerking a thumb in the direction of the low, red sports-car, 'is a very expensive one!'

'Expensive?' she said blankly. What was he talking about? What had that to do with anything? 'Please let go of me.' She added these words softly, her eyes never moving from his. She had no idea how vacant her own eyes looked. Vacant but extremely beautiful, misted slightly as they were with tears which were not yet ready to come.

The man's mouth tightened, his lips thinning into a straight line as his eyes probed hers in vain. She felt his hand tremble slightly as his grip hardened even further, causing the realisation somewhere in the back of her mind that she must have given him quite a scare. 'Yes, expensive! What I'm saying is that I don't want its paintwork ruined by the blood and broken bones of some female drowned rat who's decided she's tired of living. Got it? If that is the case with you, then I suggest you do the job properly and walk under a nice, big, bulbous bus whose brakes aren't likely to be as keen as mine are!'

Ruth still wasn't shocked. His words didn't make any sense at all to her, left her completely unmoved. 'Excuse me,' she said, turning, and with one long last look at her, the man let her go.

The department store was one of those which sold everything, a privately owned place which was not the biggest in town but one of quality. On the ground floor, at the rear, was the food department. At the front, near the cosmetics and jewellery sections, were the stands where cards of every description were sold.

It was to this section Ruth headed after buying her groceries. Had it not been written on to her shopping list two days ago, she would never have remembered to buy a birthday card for one of the girls at work. Not today. She wasn't thinking at all. The lights in the store were dazzling her, the voices of other shoppers sounding abnormally loud in her ears as she scanned the racks of birthday cards in front of her. Any card would do, as long as it was vaguely appropriate.

As she picked one up, a sharp pain stabbed at her temple and at that same instant she saw that she was wearing her engagement ring. She gasped at the sight of it, she had put it on automatically when dressing, just as she'd automatically put on her watch. But she wasn't entitled to wear the ring any more, was she? She wasn't engaged any longer. Garry wasn't coming back to her. They would never buy that lovely little house, never know the joy of choosing furnishings for it . . .

'Miss? Excuse me——'

She turned to see a teenage boy smiling at her, handing her a shopping bag which looked vaguely familiar. 'You forgot this. It is yours, isn't it?'

'I—oh, yes. Thank you, I was . . .' She never finished the sentence. She took her bag from the boy, dropped the birthday card into it and glanced again at her shopping list. She had finished. Everything listed had been bought.

With a sense of relief she headed for the door, knowing a sudden desire to get out of the overheated store, away from the hubbub of voices and piped music. Once on the street she took a deep breath and tried very hard to remember where the bus-stop was. She felt dizzy, light-headed, the cold damp air was affecting her strangely.

'Excuse me——'

Ruth heard the words again and this time she knew they were directed at her because a hand fell heavily on to her shoulder and effectively stopped her in her tracks. Surely it wasn't him again, the man in the red car? The angry one. Or was it the teenage boy? Had she done something stupid again?

She turned to see a woman of middle age, a stout, surly-faced female with cold, codfish eyes, a woman who told her very clearly what she had done . . .

The following hour was one Ruth would never, ever, forget. Being accused of shoplifting was something she had never experienced before and although in the larger scheme of things it should have been far less worrying than anything else which had happened to her that day, it was not. It was devastating. Even though she knew she would sort it out, make this hard-faced woman see her mistake, she was panicking inwardly. Soon she was panicking outwardly, too. The store detective informed her—insisted—Ruth must go with her to the Manager's office, at which point Ruth started talking more forcefully, more rapidly than she ever had in her life.

It made no difference. She was marched to the lift by the store detective.

The awful shock of what was happening brought her more alert than she would have been even on a normal day. She registered everything now, the looks she was getting from other people as she continued protesting, the weight of her shopping bag, her saturated hair and its scruffiness and, most shocking of all, the signs which were dotted here and there in the store, signs which were all too easy to read: *Shoplifters Will Be Prosecuted*.

Then she was in a lift going up, up beyond the sales floors to the administration offices, to the Manager's office. In her hand was the birthday card—no, there were *two* birthday cards! Two, their cellophane wrappings having stuck together.

'All right,' she conceded. 'So there are two cards. You still can't think I'm the sort of person who steals! For the sake of two birthday cards? You can't be serious! Good grief, I've just spent twenty-odd pounds in your grocery department—look, here's my receipt for the money. I paid cash. I—I just wasn't thinking when I put that card in my bag, honestly! I didn't mean to walk out without paying for it! Look, why don't you just let me pay you for it—for them—now?'

It was useless. She went on and on, begging the woman to let her pay for the cards, begging her to let her go, apologising, explaining, but all to no avail. The store detective would not be budged. She merely repeated that she was acting in accordance with her instructions and that the store's policy ... the store's policy ...

Heaven help her, Ruth knew what the store's policy was but she could not conceive of it happening to her. Surely they didn't, wouldn't, prosecute for something so small? For the supposed theft of two birthday cards? It was incredible.

But it was happening.

Everything was happening too fast, like in a bad dream when one finds oneself first in one setting then suddenly in another. She was walking along carpeted corridors now, hearing the noise of typewriters, voices, doors opening and closing, the chink of a teaspoon against a cup. The next thing she knew, she was sitting in an office, an outer office, presumably that of the manager's secretary.

Her mind was spinning in utter bewilderment. This couldn't really be happening, could it? Dear God, she'd lose her job if they carried out their 'policy'! She would never be able to set foot outside her front door again. Oh, the shame of it! It would be all over the local paper . . . her parents would have a fit . . .

'Would you come this way, please?' She turned to find a young woman speaking to her. At her side stood the detective, who had never moved away from Ruth since first accosting her in the street.

She and the matronly woman followed the secretary into an office overlooking the busy street where she had almost walked under the car and for one insane moment she almost wished she had been hit by that car. If that had happened, she wouldn't be here now, in this store. In this ridiculous, impossible situation.

There was nobody in the office and the secretary looked nonplussed. 'Oh. Er—Mr Bell must have slipped out for a moment. Take a seat, please. He'll be right with you.'

With an impassive, imperturbable face, the detective sat and gestured for Ruth to do the same. She ignored her, knowing it was pointless to try to explain herself all over again. Instead she went to stand by the window and kept her eyes on the rain which was belting against it, trembling and hoping against hope that the Store Manager would be more reasonable. He had to be, he just had to be! He would have to listen to and believe her explanation!

At the sound of the door opening, she spun round almost frantically to face the man who would decide her fate. Immediately, she knew a sickening, sinking sensation in her stomach, knew it was hopeless, absolutely hopeless! In the doorway of a communicating office he stood, staring at her with a disbelief clearly equal to her own.

It was him, the man in the red sports car.

His heavy black brows were pulled together in a frown and his deep blue eyes bored into her, making her feel guilty in spite of her innocence. 'I—look, I want—'

She got no further than that. The man spoke at the same time, glancing in the direction of the store detective as he did so. 'Excuse me,' he muttered. 'I didn't realise there was someone in here. Where's Geoff—Mr Bell? He was here a moment ago.'

The older woman looked at him without a trace of recognition, without a hint of emotion. 'We're waiting for him. He's on his way, so I believe. I suggest you have a word with his secretary.'

The man retreated but not before he had slid his eyes very carefully over the square-shouldered matron, then in turn over Ruth, who was fixed to the spot by the window. She couldn't move a muscle. All she knew was tremendous relief that this particular man was not the Store Manager. Her glimmer of hope rekindled itself. If she'd had to explain herself to this granite-faced giant, she'd have been doomed.

In the seconds before he took his eyes from her, he said gruffly, 'I have the impression you've landed yourself in trouble again.' He glanced meaningfully at the detective as though he recognised exactly what she was.

He closed the door as he retreated, leaving Ruth open-mouthed at his spitefulness. What a stupid thing to say! Fancy saying she'd landed herself in trouble again! What would the detective make of *that*?

It was something she never learned the answer to. Within minutes Mr Bell appeared, a smart, pleasant-faced man in his early forties who immediately started to sort things out.

'Now, Mrs Nichols, what seems to be the problem?'

Ruth and her captor started talking simultaneously and for several seconds, chaos reigned. Mr Bell didn't even look at Ruth, let alone listen to her, all his concentration was on the detective and what she was telling him. She told how she'd been watching Ruth on the ground floor, how she'd picked up several pieces of jewellery on her way to the card department, looked at them and replaced them. 'I've been through the contents of her bags and there are two birthday cards which haven't been paid for.' She spoke detachedly enough, was truthful to the letter and yet somehow her words managed to insinuate a great deal. It was as if she were convinced Ruth had considered pinching some jewellery as well. Ruth couldn't even remember having touched any jewellery but she couldn't deny that she had because she'd been in such a dream, such a daze, she might well have looked at a few things, idly, unthinkingly.

Still, she'd had no thought of taking something, anything, without paying for it and she would say so in no uncertain terms! 'Mr Bell, if I might just be allowed to explain——'

'One moment, please.' Again the Manager cut her off, again he did not look at her. He looked straight at the other employee and asked her to leave the room.

Mrs Nichols was clearly surprised at being asked to leave. Whether this was or was not the store's policy, the way things were normally handled, Ruth had no way of knowing. She knew only a sense of relief when the cod-eyed detective got up and left the office. Nevertheless, she was white-faced as she turned to the Manager with huge, frightened eyes. 'Mr Bell——'

'Sit down, Miss . . .? May I have your name, please? Your full name and your address.'

'My—I . . .' Confused, Ruth sat. Conflicting information was coming at her. He wanted her name and address but—but he was smiling at her, his voice was kindly and he assured her this was just a matter of routine. 'What do you mean? You're not going to call the police or something?'

'No. I think we can sort this out ourselves, don't you?'

She certainly hoped so. She gave him her name and address without further question and immediately went on to tell him of the state she'd been in. Babbling, she told him she'd had a terrible shock that morning, plus some very bad news which was also shocking, but she did not go into detail. She would have, gladly, had the man seemed unconvinced. But he did not. He looked at her evenly, nodding as she talked, then to her astonishment he told her she could go.

'*Go*? I can go?'

It was later, much later before she realised quite how perverse human nature can be at times. She had been told she could go, get out of that humiliating situation merely by walking away from it, yet it had all seemed too easy. There she had been, so determined to fight, so well rehearsed with her answers by the time she got the chance to speak up—yet the questions had not been forthcoming. Mr Bell had merely said there was obviously a misunderstanding, she could forget the incident, and that had been that.

Naturally she had been relieved, indescribably so. But she doubted she could forget the incident. Ever.

CHAPTER TWO

'You were lucky.'

Ruth stared at her brother. She really didn't have a temper but this statement from Derek brought a hot flush to her cheeks. 'Lucky? You say I was lucky after that woman had the nerve to pick me up for shoplifting? Lucky? After the humiliation I went through? Do you realise how much it would have cost me if I'd been prosecuted? My job, my pride, my good name——'

'Yes, all of that, probably. But it didn't happen. The Store Manager clearly had no intention of prosecuting you. He had one over-zealous detective on his hands and one temporarily demented customer. He could have taken it further but he let you off without even a warning. He knew it was a genuine mistake on your part. That's what I meant by lucky. You were lucky he was human enough to do what he did with you.'

'Oh,' Ruth wanted to cry again. She had been with Wendy and Derek at their house in Dagenham for almost a week and was taking the train home tomorrow. God, how she hated the thought of going in to work on Monday. There would be so many questions about the absence of her engagement ring . . .

She looked over at Wendy, who was smiling sympathetically while nodding in agreement with her husband. Wendy, who was fair-haired and quite short in stature, was very different from Ruth both physically and in personality. Wendy was bubbly, outgoing, whereas Ruth was backward in coming forward. She was a generous girl, Wendy, generous of self. Poor Wendy, it was she who had done the comforting since she'd been out of hospital, not Ruth. It was Wendy who had encouraged Ruth to talk. As soon as she'd set eyes on her, she'd known something was terribly wrong. Derek had, too, but to neither of them had Ruth said anything for two whole days. She'd asked them not to question her, explaining that she'd tell them what was wrong as soon as she was able to. For two days she had been living on the brink of tears, feeling unable to tell them anything at all in case she started crying and was unable to stop. She had kept the news of Garry's letter to herself until she thought she had enough control to be able to talk about it without breaking down.

After being with her relatives for a couple of days, she had managed to tell them about it. But she had cried after all, almost from the beginning of her first sentence. Only then had she taken off her engagement ring, in front of them, relieved that the pretence was over. Very deliberately she had removed the ring and put it carefully in the small box in her handbag. 'I can take this off now. I kept on wearing it because I didn't want you or anyone else to suspect what was wrong. I've . . . I've been unable to tell anyone until now, you see.'

They had both looked at her with tenderness, both understanding what others might consider odd behaviour.

When she got back to Wolverhampton she would take the ring to Garry's parents. She didn't want it. She would leave it in their safe keeping to give to their son when he got home from Saudi. Let him give it to Angela, his new love.

Aware of the bitterness in her thoughts, her heart, Ruth tried to stop it. She mustn't allow herself to be bitter, it was unhealthy. But I've been jilted! she thought in the next instant. Aren't I entitled to be bitter? Garry and I had a good life ahead of us, a bright future planned very carefully. And now what? What was she going to *do*? It was going to be so embarrassing at work, so embarrassing to have to tell them . . .

She hadn't even been able to tell Mrs Edwards, her neighbour, when she'd taken Tabatha round to her house to be looked after for these few days. That was why she'd kept the ring on her finger. She hadn't been able to face questions at that point. With Derek and Wendy it had been comparatively easy, not only did they love her, they understood her very well indeed, far better than her own parents, even. Oh, what would they say? What would her parents say when she told them?

She wanted to run away. Childishly, all she could think of right now was how good it would be to stay here for a while, with her brother and his wife. But that was impossible. She had to be at work on Monday and it would be a busy week. An awful week. Wendy had already suggested she stay on for a while, for as long as she liked, in fact, but she couldn't.

There had been one good point during the past week, though. Wendy had been examined by a specialist the previous day and informed that there was, indeed, something physically amiss. She had been told that her womb was slightly retroverted and that an operation would put it right. There should, she had been promised, be no problem with pregnancy in the future.

That had been more than a good spot, it had been joyous news. Wendy, an optimist in any case, had not been as depressed as Ruth had expected to find her. But now, now she was completely her old self again. She had hope again. Real hope.

'Ruth? Where've you gone? Are you still vexed because I said you were lucky? You were, you know.'

She smiled at her brother. ''Course I'm not vexed. How can I stay vexed with you? It's myself I'm angry with. How could I have been so stupid? I can see myself right now, putting those birthday cards into my bag without remembering to pay for them. All I knew was that a card was the last thing on my shopping list and I had to get out of that overheated store. Now I'll never be able to go in the place again.'

'You're such a worrier!' Derek got up to pour more coffee for everyone. 'Why on earth shouldn't you shop there again?'

'Don't be daft. If that detective woman ever spotted me, she'd watch me like a hawk. I couldn't bear it. I feel like a criminal as it is.'

'Well, you're not,' Wendy said firmly. 'So stop being silly. I find the episode with the car far more alarming. From the sound of it, you were almost under its wheels.'

Ruth shrugged. She'd now told Wendy and Derek everything about last Saturday, including her episode with the man in the car and the way he had popped up suddenly in the Store Manager's office. But she had thought no more about that. That had been the least traumatic of all, just one of those things.

Failing her driving test hadn't worried her, either. She hadn't expected to pass it, not when her mind had been so distracted by thoughts of Garry. Garry. She would probably never see him again. At least, she hoped she wouldn't.

By the middle of the following week, Ruth had exactly the same thought again—for the hundredth time. She never wanted to set eyes on Garry Anderson again. Her bitterness was becoming more and more difficult to keep in check. Never before had she been one of those women who said, 'Men!' in a disgusted tone. Not that there had been many men in her life. There could have been, oh, there could have been, she was always being asked out. Even the engagement ring hadn't stopped the offers from being made. Unaware of her own attractiveness, she had always been at a loss to see why men were drawn to her.

Garry had been the first serious relationship in her life, not the longest lasting but certainly the most serious. She had grown to love him in a fairly short time because he had the special qualities she wanted in a man, tenderness, understanding, sensitivity. They had also wanted the same things out of life, the same sort of life, children, a nice home, a good, steady . . .

Oh, what was the point? It was over, *over*. And now she almost hated Garry. She hated him for the humiliation he had caused her, a humiliation which seemed unending. Everyone at work knew now, her neighbours knew, her parents knew. They had phoned to see how she was getting on and she had told them, seeing no point in waiting for them to get home before she broke the news. It would give them time to adjust. Perhaps by the time they got back to England, some of the shock would have worn off.

If only she could say the same for herself, she was so depressed she was thinking of handing in her notice, was thinking very seriously of moving away. Maybe she would go and live in Australia? Stay with her sister Helen until she found a job and a place to live? No, no, that was a silly idea. Australia had never appealed to her.

What about moving down south? She could stay with Derek and Wendy. Finding a job would be no problem down there. Wendy had worked in an employment agency until she got pregnant and had to rest, which was right from the start. She had friends in the agency, with Ruth's qualifications they would be sure to find something suitable for her.

The more she thought about it, the more the idea appealed to her. There was no reason at all for staying in Wolverhampton now. Indeed, there was every reason to get away. Almost everything she did, everywhere she went, reminded her of Garry. Even when she walked past the cinema she thought of him, of the way they would sit always in the same row, arguing who would fetch the ice creams during the interval. Garry had never shared her love of poetry but apart from that one thing, they had had so much in common, how could this have happened? How could he go away and in the space of five months be in love with someone else? It couldn't be real, his new love, it simply couldn't be.

She hadn't sent him a reply to his letter, there was no need. The very absence of a reply would be his acknowledgement. Besides, she wouldn't have known what to say.

On the Thursday before her parents were due home, Ruth rang her brother and told him that not only was she going to move in with him for a few weeks, she was actually thinking of moving to the area for good. 'At least, I'd like to see how I feel about Essex, see whether I'd like to live there after I've been there a few weeks. Could you stand it, Derek? Could you put up with me for a bit? I could work as a temp and——'

And it was arranged there and then. There wasn't, as she had known there wouldn't be, any problem as far as Derek and Wendy were concerned. Not only were they delighted, they thought her very wise. They said that a complete change was just what she needed.

Ruth hoped they were right. The way she felt now

was awful, she was listless and uninterested in anything. She felt depressed and as though she'd aged ten years in a matter of weeks. Most of all she felt disorientated, as if her future had been wiped away. Yet she had years ahead of her. Years she did not quite know what to do with.

CHAPTER THREE

'HAVE you got something for me for next week, Jan?'

Ruth sat down at Jan's desk in the employment
agency in the centre of Dagenham. She had called in
to collect her pay and to see what was cooking for the
following week. She had been temping for just under
two months and hadn't been without work so far.

They had been right, Derek and Wendy. Being here
had helped enormously. She liked what she had seen
so far of Essex, she liked the town and she loved living
in her brother's new, four-bedroomed, detached
house. It was far grander than the terraced house she'd
lived in with her parents. Of course, she would have to
get used to something much more modest when she
found her own place. She was looking for a place on
her own already. Much as she loved being with her
relatives, and they loved having her, Ruth was wise
enough to know she shouldn't outstay her welcome.

Everything had worked out well so far, though.
Wendy had had her operation privately and had had
Ruth there to look after her during the day while
Derek was at work. Only when she had completely
recovered did Ruth start temping.

'Actually, there's not much at the moment', said
Jan.

Ruth looked up in surprise. 'You're joking, surely?'

The other girl shook her head. 'Things have been
very quiet this week, for some reason.' She was
shuffling through some cards, frowning. 'I have got
something—for a receptionist with some typing.
These people really want a permanent. They've had a

30

series of temps and they've been interviewing but they haven't found anyone suitable. Or so they say. Seem very fussy if you ask me, though they are offering a good salary.' She shrugged. 'It's yours if you want it, Ruth. It might last a week, it might last several. Depends when they find themselves someone permanant. But you're overqualified for it.'

'I'll take it.' Ruth spoke without preamble, unconcerned about being overqualified. She wasn't even bothered about the money, though she did mention it. 'Will it be at a lower rate?'

'No, same rate. The usual.'

That was gratifying, though not of paramount importance. It was just that she was thinking of buying a flat. She'd looked at three, one of which was available for rent, two of which were for sale. It was Derek who'd suggested she buy rather than rent, pointing out to her that renting was a bad idea, that a place of her own would be an investment. It made sense, of course. Derek always made sense. At thirty-one, he was sensible and successful, wise when it came to matters of finance. It was his job.

That was something Ruth had never been, capable with money. She had never saved in her life until . . . until Garry. Then she had saved with a vengeance, putting money every week into the Building Society account, just as he had.

On moving to Essex she had transferred her money into a branch in Dagenham. But this time it was in her name only. She had taken exactly that which she had put into the joint account in Wolverhampton, not a penny more, not a penny less. Of course, she had taken more than she had left in the account because she had the five thousand pounds from her Premium Bonds. Yes, she could afford to buy a flat here. She could put down a substantial deposit and handle a

mortgage, within reason. Derek had already worked
everything out for her. But she was dithering, was not
exactly relishing the idea of living on her own.

'It's a nine-o'clock start,' Jan was telling her. 'Five-
thirty finish, but there's an hour and a half for lunch
It's convenient for you, too, you can get the bus right
on the corner of Wendy's road.'

Ruth frowned. 'You mean it isn't in town?'

'No, it's much nearer where you're living, it's on a
new industrial estate about halfway between
Dagenham and Ilford, it's near Becontree.'

'I know it.' Ruth nodded. The flat she was
thinking of buying was in Becontree, not too far from
her brother's house but just a little further away from
Dagenham itself. 'What sort of place is it?'

Jan glanced at the card she was holding. 'Toy
manufacturers, it's Marsden Toys.'

Ruth's eyebrows rose slightly. Marsden Toys, she'd
heard of them. They weren't exactly a household name
but she had a strong feeling they made those gorgeous,
soft, cuddly toys she'd looked at last Christmas when
she'd been shopping for something to send to her
niece in Australia. She thanked Jan for her trouble and
left.

'It doesn't quite sound like your scene,' Derek said
over dinner that evening. 'An industrial estate?
Factories and all? And a job as a receptionist? You'll
probably be bored out of your mind. Receptionists sit
filing their nails all day, don't they?'

'What a nerve!' Wendy laughed at him. 'The one at
your office might but——' She broke off when she
caught the twinkle in her husband's eye. 'Anyway,'
she went on, looking at Ruth, 'we'll drive past the
estate tonight, make sure you know exactly where it is.'

'Oh . . . yes.' Ruth had forgotten she was going to
look again at the flat she fancied.

Wendy caught the hesitation, frowning. 'Aren't you sure, Ruth? About that flat? Look, don't let Derek talk you into buying it if you're not absolutely sure.'

'I am. I mean, I—I am sure about the flat. I mean, I like it very much and it's a good buy, what with the present owners leaving all the carpets and the cooker and whatnot but——'

'But?'

How could she say it when it might sound childish? The truth was she didn't fancy the idea of living on her own.

'Ruth?' It was her brother. 'You've vanished again, always drifting off into your own thoughts! You've never grown out of that, have you? My dreamy sister! Penny for them? Is it the responsibility that's worrying you? The financial responsibility? I know you've always been a drip when it comes to handling money but you can manage this easily, you know—as long as you don't spend as much on clothes as you used to. I'll say that much for Garry—he curbed your spending for you.'

Wendy shot him a look of disgust. 'How very tactful! Not only do you criticise her for being thoughtful, you also call her a drip and you remind her of that stinker.' She turned to Ruth, a look of worry on her face. 'I know what's bothering you, it's the idea of living alone, isn't it?'

Ruth nodded reluctantly. This was the top and bottom of it.

'Then don't. Stay here, with us. There's bags of room here and you know Derek and I love having you. Take no notice of him and his teasing, he's still your big brother with your best interests at heart.'

Ruth knew that. And how typical this was of her sister-in-law. But it wasn't on, she couldn't stay with them for ever and she said as much. 'Nor can I go back to Mum and Dad. I don't want to live in Wolverhampton any more and besides, it's high time I left the nest. Theirs and yours.' Sighing, she looked at Wendy with a sadness she was unaware of. 'So it looks as though it's decision time for me, mm?'

'Ruth, forgive me for saying so but ... well, Derek and I have both been concerned about you ever since you came here. You've had no social life at all—absolutely none. You haven't even been out to the cinema. I—we think——'

'What she's trying to say,' Derek intervened, his own face creased with worry, 'is that you're twenty-two years old, single and gorgeous. Now there's an admission for you!' he added, grinning. 'There are plenty more fish in the sea. You might be uninterested at the moment but that's no reason why you shouldn't go out and enjoy yourself, even if it's with other girls. You can't tell us you haven't been invited out—by both sexes. You've met enough people in those offices where you've been temping. And what about your driving lessons? You said you'd have some and take another test, but you haven't even done anything about that.'

They meant well, both of them. She wasn't going to tell them she had no real enthusiasm for anything, men, outings, driving lessons, flats or anything else. If she admitted as much they would only nag her more, albeit in their kind way. 'You're right,' she said instead. 'It's time I pulled myself together.'

Ruth tried pulling herself together that very evening by committing herself to the purchase of the one-bedroomed flat in Becontree. The following morning, Saturday, she went into the Building Society and set the financial ball rolling. The only real enthusiasm she had, though, was for the idea that as soon as she had her own place, she would go home and collect

Tabatha. She missed that cat as much as she missed the man she'd been planning to marry. It was a startling thought but it was the truth.

At five minutes to nine on Monday morning she reached the end of the rather long walk which took her from the bus-stop to the entrance of Marsden Toys. The layout of the place was clear to see, there was a small factory to the rear of an office block over which there was a large sign in bold letters. It read: 'Marsden Toys Ltd' and underneath that it said: 'Marsden Executive Gifts Ltd'. The executive gifts, whatever that meant, came as news to Ruth.

She walked through two sets of double glass doors and found herself in the reception area. Not surprisingly, there was nobody behind the desk but on it there was a small brass bell and a sign saying, 'Please ring for attention.' She did. A few seconds later a smartly dressed female appeared, a woman of about thirty years who was wearing a navy blue suit which was beautifully cut and teamed with a crisp, white blouse.

Both women smiled before a word was spoken. Ruth was dressed almost identically, even their shoes were similar, navy blue and plain, medium heeled.

It was a little odd, actually, the way they both surveyed one another before uttering a word. They were both tall, black-haired, lightly but expertly made-up, but there was an air of confidence about the older woman which Ruth did not share. She was by no means nervous but never in her life had she exuded the sort of self-assurance this person was blessed with.

Five minutes later Ruth was sitting in the office of Dinah Marsden, drinking coffee and being put in the picture.

'This is an expanding company, Ruth. Recently,

we've gone into executive toys and gifts, as well as the children's toys which we manufacture ourselves. There are three Directors, myself and my younger brother, Rory. He's responsible for most of our sales and salesmen. I do the hiring and firing, handle day-to-day staff problems and a dozen other things, whatever's necessary to help out where I'm needed.' She shrugged, as if slightly amused by her definition of her own role.

Ruth liked her. She couldn't say why, she just did, from the start. There were no rings on her fingers, she was in no way affected, she was friendly and natural and spoke in a clear, unaccented voice. Her black hair was short and curled softly around her face in a style which flattered her. She was, Ruth thought detachedly, very attractive with alert, positive blue eyes and a fine bone-structure.

She was unsure why, as a temp, she should be given this somewhat detailed run-down about the company, but she listened with interest.

'My older brother is Chairman and Managing Director and his function——' she paused, smiling. 'Blake is jack of all trades and master of all of them, too. Unfortunately he's away at the moment on a buying trip in Japan—the executive gifts side of the business. That's his baby. He also designs the children's toys we manufacture. He and our cutter, whom you'll meet in due course.' She paused again, surveying Ruth openly. 'Pity Blake's away, I hope you're still here when he gets back, which will be in about three weeks. We're looking for someone permanent, actually, and I've interviewed quite a number of people.'

Ruth nodded, saying nothing. Why was Dinah being so careful about choosing someone for a receptionist's job? Surely the ability to type and look presentable was enough? She got an answer to this quite unexpectedly. In fact it was almost as though Dinah Marsden had read her mind.

'It's quite difficult, to be honest. We're looking for a secretary-cum-receptionist, really. Bit awkward. We need someone who can do my typing, which doesn't amount to much, and handle the overspill from Blake. He has a secretary but—well, with things getting busier almost by the week, it's getting to be more than Millie can handle.'

Millie. By the end of that week, Ruth had got to know Millie O'Brian quite well. Irish right down to her fingertips, she was petite and blonde and had a dynamic personality. Ruth had never seen anyone type as fast in all her years in offices. She had a delightful, Southern Irish brogue and she came out with the most unlikely prefixes to some of her sentences. Yet (and Ruth hated to think this because it seemed catty) she just didn't seem to be the sort of material Managing Directors' secretaries were made of. This was a go-ahead, expanding firm which had lots of callers, many of whom were, of course, customers, and Millie seemed ... rather rough and ready. Some days she was made-up, some days she wasn't. Her shoes always looked as if they needed cleaning. Smart, she wasn't. Efficient, she was. A breath of fresh air, she most certainly was! She was very, very likable and she obviously thought extremely highly of her absent boss.

By the end of her second week, Ruth had met everyone except some of those who worked in the factory; she had met some but not all of them when she'd been shown around by the warehouse/factory manager. Dinah's younger brother, Rory, was as attractive as she in a boyish sort of way. He struck Ruth as boyish despite his age. He was twenty-eight and a born flirt, Ruth learned from Millie. 'Not half the character his older brother is,' she also learned from Millie. To be sure.

During the middle of her third week, Ruth was offered the job permanently. She didn't even hesitate, to her own surprise. She had so enjoyed the informal, friendly atmosphere, the busyness of the place, the varied jobs she'd been doing. What did it matter if she were overqualified? She liked the place! And the people! The salary was good, too, and since she would soon be paying a mortgage off, a permanent job was something she needed. Also it would be so very convenient to get to from where her new flat was.

She said all of this when Dinah raised her brows, surprised at her rapid acceptance.

'You don't want to think it over?'

'There's no need.'

'I must caution you that things will hot up considerably when Blake gets back. Take my word!'

'I'm not exactly overworked now, am I?' Ruth laughed. 'What's the matter, Dinah, are you trying to talk me out of it?'

'Absolutely not!' The older woman held up a hand. 'I'm very impressed with you, that's the truth. You're accurate, neat, conscientious, punctual, you have a perfect telephone manner and you're extremely good to look at.'

Feeling vaguely embarrassed, Ruth blinked at the compliment. It did cross her mind that perhaps she shouldn't accept the job permanently until she had met Blake Marsden, since she would be handling some of his work. But why worry? If she got on with him as well as she got on with his brother and sister, there would be no problem at all. And I will, she told herself. Why ever not?

'So it's settled?'

Recognising that this was her cue to leave Dinah's

office, Ruth got to her feet and held out her hand. 'It's settled.' She didn't need to say more; she was sufficiently familiar with Dinah's routine to know she would get an official letter offering the job, to which she would give an official reply.

Neither she nor Dinah could have had any inkling that disaster was about to strike. Neither she nor Dinah could have guessed that Ruth's face would be a familiar and unwelcome one to the company Chairman and Managing Director. Everything had been so neatly stitched up and settled by the time Mr Blake Marsden came back from Japan, which was on the Tuesday of Ruth's fourth week with the company. Of course, she had no idea who he was when he walked into reception.

It was a beautiful, sunny, early June morning. She was sitting, as usual, at the large, semi-circular desk in reception, a plush, comfortable room whose walls were partly shelved to house a display of soft toys. Huge photographs of dolls, teddies and various other items were also on display; there were several leather chairs, a square coffee-table on which there were trade magazines, and on Ruth's desk there was an electric typewriter and the switchboard she had long since mastered.

It was into this setting he walked, just before lunchtime, a tall, broad, unsmiling man whose face she recognised immediately. He was out of context; three months had passed since she had seen him and he was miles away from the city in which she'd done so, but she had not forgotten. Not only had the circumstances of their first meeting been traumatic for her, he himself was unforgettable not only because of his striking looks but mainly because of that overbearing, arrogant attitude of his.

When he swung his way confidently through the

double glass doors, Ruth was so taken aback that she rose from her seat, staring at him in instant recognition. For what seemed like minutes, she couldn't speak, could do no more than gape at him.

Blake Marsden was doing likewise. It was he who spoke first. 'What the devil are you doing here?' he demanded.

'I—I work here,' she mumbled. Was he a customer? A sales rep? What on earth was he doing here, at Marsden Toys? Her mind was so busy speculating, she simply wasn't thinking straight. Her next words were hardly appropriate, especially when he might well have been a customer. Quite curtly, she asked, 'And what are you doing here?'

Those memorable blue eyes dug into her face, as cold and deep as a wintry sea. One heavy black eyebrow rose sardonically and his mean mouth twisted in a parody of a smile. 'Oh, I just happen to own the place,' he said.

CHAPTER FOUR

RUTH couldn't believe her ears. 'You—you're Blake Marsden?' She had walked so often past the door bearing this man's name, she had been in his office more than a dozen times, she'd handled his papers, his belongings, even his telephone, but never, never had it crossed her mind that she had already met the big boss.

Groaning inwardly, she sank on to her chair, his critical, supercilious look making her feel like something lower than a worm. She found herself avoiding his eyes. This was the man whose car she had very nearly walked under that awful, unforgettable day in Wolverhampton. This was the man who had appeared again in the Manager's office of the store where she had been suspected, *accused*, of shoplifting. And he had known, as sure as eggs were eggs he had known what she was doing in that room, being watched over by that horrible woman.

'And you are?'

She still couldn't look at him. With absolute certainty she knew this would be her last day in the job she was enjoying so much. 'Ruth Boyd.'

'Well, Ruth Boyd, you're a long way from Wolverhampton.' He spoke so sharply in that deep, gruff voice of his that her eyes lifted involuntarily. Even the voice was something she remembered clearly. 'Would you mind telling me how long you've been here? You're a temp, I suppose? Yet another.'

'I—almost a month. I started as a temp and your sister——'

As if on cue, Dinah walked in to reception at that instant. 'Blake! How lovely! When did you get back?' Not waiting for an answer, she went over to her brother and planted a kiss on his cheek. Ruth watched, half-convinced the man would push his sister aside. He looked thoroughly disgruntled.

Dinah pulled a face, touched her fingers to her lips. 'You need a shave, love.'

'I've driven straight from the airport,' he said by way of explanation. 'Get someone to bring the boxes from the boot of my car, Di. They're hefty, better get one of the lads from the warehouse.'

'Certainly.' Smiling, which was something Dinah did easily and often, she turned to Ruth, 'Ruth, meet our Chairman and MD, my brother——'

'We've met.' The words came from Blake. At his sister's look of enquiry, he said more clearly, 'Miss Boyd and I have met.'

Only Ruth knew he was referring to the past, not that they had known one another's names at the time. Dinah thought he meant they had just introduced themselves and set eyes on each other for the first time.

When the pair of them disappeared into the inner sanctum of offices, Ruth stared despairingly at nothing. All that would rapidly change, of course. How long would it take, how long before she was called in to Dinah's office and questioned about the incident in the store in Wolverhampton?

She braced herself, unsure whether she was prepared to go through the long explanation of all that had happened that day. She had passed on to Dinah the glowing reference she'd been given by her ex-boss at the Building Society; she had supplied a character reference, too, but the shoplifting episode would still have to be explained satisfactorily. How to begin? And did she want to explain everything? It was too . . . too personal, too painful. Nobody here knew anything about Garry Anderson or her personal circumstances—except that she was living with her brother and moving in to her own flat at the end of the month. She didn't want anyone here knowing about her past. She wanted to forget the past.

But it had been resurrected. The moment Blake Marsden had walked into sight, the past had come rushing at her like snatches from a horror film. Even now she was going red in the face. She could feel it happening to her as she re-lived those terrible minutes in that department store.

The internal telephone buzzed. Ruth closed her eyes. This was it, she just knew it. Hired and fired within the space of one month. It would be a first for her.

But it wasn't Dinah, it was himself. Himself. Ruth had picked that up from his secretary. Millie almost always referred to her boss as 'himself', not in a disparaging way, far from it. Her admiration for her boss had been clear from the outset.

Well, Ruth thought, it takes all sorts.

'Yes, Mr Marsden?'

'Come to my office, Miss Boyd. Straight away.' He hung up before she could say anything.

She was nervous now, more nervous than she could remember being for many years. Since she was in school, since that time she had been summoned to the Head Mistress's office, having been reported by her form teacher for dancing in the corridors . . .

What an idiot she was! What did it matter if she had to leave here? Finding a job would be no problem at all for her.

Catching sight of herself in the glass doors, she smoothed down the skirt of the cherry-red dress she was wearing. Her hair was tumbling around her shoulders, as she always wore it, but it needed combing. Well, it probably needed combing. She sat down again and fished in her bag for her comb and her compact, delaying the confrontation with Blake Marsden. *Why* was she feeling so utterly disappointed? So what if this place was easy to get to from her new home? She could find another job locally.

But it wasn't that. Not really. Well, it was partly that. Yes, it was convenient for her here, yes she liked the people and the work. What was bothering her mainly though was her pride. If she had had the game, she wouldn't mind having the name. But she was innocent! She had done nothing whatsoever to deserve what was coming!

'Millie? Shall I just go in, or what?'

Millie was pulling on her cardigan, getting her things together. So she was still going home for lunch; it obviously made no difference that her boss was back. Every day, she collected her six-year-old twins from school and took them home for lunch. This was something Ruth admired about her, something she thought charming, her seeing her children at lunch-time. Millie had said she did this because it broke up the day for them. 'It also eases my conscience because I work full time. Where I was brought up, women with six-year-old kids didn't go out to work full time, if at all.' She had shrugged, seemingly vaguely unhappy with herself. 'But I need the money. My husband's been out of work for over a year. Besides, I've worked for himself since before I was married, can't imagine life without him!'

Ruth hadn't known whether to take that seriously. Millie was like that, one couldn't always be sure whether she was joking or not.

'Millie?' She looked to her for guidance now. 'I've been summoned, shall I go straight in?'

'You'd better.' On this occasion, it was very obvious she was serious. 'He's in one of his moods.'

'His moods?' Was she the cause of it? Ruth wondered.

'Saints preserve us!' Millie looked heavenward. 'Jet lag—or whatever they call it. It'll be worse tomorrow.' Laughing at the look on Ruth's face, she added, 'But don't worry. He'll be normal again by the end of the week.'

Normal? What was that, exactly?

With a wave at Millie, Ruth knocked tentatively on the communicating door. There was no answer. All she could hear was a faint buzzing sound she couldn't identify.

She knocked harder.

The sound stopped. Blake Marsden's voice barked at her to come in.

Ruth crossed the threshold without further ado, cursing herself for feeling just as she'd felt when the Head Mistress had sent for her. The difference was that on this occasion there was nobody behind the imposing desk. Her eyes moved swiftly around the room, reflecting her confusion. Then, gasping, she spotted him.

He was standing in what she had thought was a cupboard of some sort, a door in the panelling on the wall. But it wasn't a cupboard, it was a small washroom in which there was a basin, a row of shelves and a small rail, hanging from which was a suit and a shirt in plastic bags.

Blake Marsden was standing at the basin, his back to her, and Ruth stared at him as though she'd never seen a man before. He was naked from the waist up.

Blinking her astonishment, she was just about to ask whether she should come back later when he spoke. 'Don't stand there gaping, Miss Boyd. Sit yourself down and get your pencil at the ready.'

'Pardon?' She was looking directly at the back of his dark head—until her eyes slid involuntarily over the broad, muscular back. Hairy, she thought with disgust. He's even got hair on his back, just beneath his lungs. What must his chest be like?

She found out very quickly. She raised her eyes to find that he was watching her in the mirror over the basin. 'What's the matter? Am I embarrassing you? I can see the whites of your eyes, lady. They're like two chocolate drops surrounded by icing.' He turned to face her, giving her the benefit of his solid, wide-shouldered chest, a chest which was indeed covered with black hair but not as thickly as she had expected it to be.

'Time,' he went on, before she could assimilate his previous words. 'I never waste it. It's too precious. Where's your notebook?'

'Pardon?'

Blake Marsden drew a long, slow breath, his lips closed firmly together and turned down at the corners in annoyance. 'My sister tells me you're now on the permanent payroll, that your work is excellent and you have the added advantage of writing shorthand.'

She could do no more than look at him, keeping her eyes carefully on his face.

'Millie doesn't. Write shorthand, I mean. She uses a dictaphone. Can you?'

'Of course.' She spoke without thinking, without even beginning to understand where this was leading.

His eyebrows rose slightly. 'Ah! A positive answer, at last. I was beginning to think you were hard of hearing, Ruth.'

She stood, facing him across the length of his office, her big brown eyes growing even wider. What was he playing at? Why didn't he get to the point and stop being so horribly sarcastic? 'Mr Marsden, would you mind telling me——'

'Blake.'

'Blake? But I thought——'

'Sit down, Ruth. Sit down and calm down.' And with that he turned back to the basin, washed his face and neck with a great deal of splashing and noise, while Ruth did as she'd been told. She sat down and she tried very hard to calm down.

Only when he had pulled on the clean shirt, buttoned it and put his tie in place did he move to his desk. He put both hands flat on the its surface and looked at her expectantly. 'You were saying?'

'I . . .' What was the use? She was getting nowhere fast. 'Mr Marsden, I thought you'd called me in here to fire me.'

'Blake,' he said again. 'Now why should I want to do that?'

She hated him in those few seconds. It was unreasonable, she knew. She hardly knew him at all. But he was just as disagreeable now as he had been when their paths had first crossed. He knew damned well why she thought her job was about to vanish, and his attitude angered her beyond description. This, in a normally placid young woman who didn't even have a temper. She lifted her head, her heart pounding ridiculously fast against her ribs. Her voice belied what was going on inside her as she spoke. Very quietly, holding the dark blue gaze of eyes which were now attractively clear, she said, 'As a matter of fact, there's no reason on earth why you should.'

'Precisely so,' he agreed, his voice equally quiet, equally firm. 'Now would you please go and get your notebook so we can get some work done? I've a lot to catch up on.'

Without question, without another word, Ruth left

the office. As soon as she closed the door behind her, she leaned against the jamb and let her eyes close. He had understood her very well. As she had understood him. The episode in Wolverhampton—both episodes, the car and the store—were not going to be referred to.

Well, hallelujah. That was very gratifying. It meant he believed her innocent. He hadn't even asked her what had happened to put her in such an awkward situation. It was a very big point in Blake Marsden's favour.

She would, she decided, stay on here.

'I'm leaving,' she thought three days later. 'I can't stand the man.'

It was only Friday and it wasn't even ten o'clock yet. Since taking dictation from him on the day he returned, Ruth had had no contact with Blake except when he'd returned the folder of letters she'd typed for him. He had signed them all except one, a letter which he'd chopped to pieces, cutting and inserting paragraphs boldly but clearly with a black-inked fountain pen. 'Do this again for me, would you, Ruth? Sorry about that.' He'd put the open folder on her desk, shifting the first letter so she could see he had signed the one beneath. 'The others are fine. An excellent job, thank you.'

She had warmed to him then. She had not gone as far as smiling at him—she'd been too taken aback to do that—but privately she had chalked up another point in his favour. So he did take time to praise his staff when they deserved it.

This morning, however, she had learned that he took time to slap them down, too. And this when they didn't deserve it!

Oh, it had been such a stupid incident! Meaningless.

Nothing! And how unfair of him to blame *her* when it was Rory's fault! If fault is what it was.

Rory Marsden was out on the road most of the time. He called in at the offices only two or three times a week, for an hour or two. Which was just as well. He fancied Ruth, she was well aware of that. He had asked her to have lunch with him the first day he met her, she had declined and that had been that. Rory had not taken offence, he was too cock-sure of himself and his good looks, too full of the confidence his sister also had. Unlike Dinah's, Rory's confidence was mildly offensive to Ruth, probably because it was too abundant, and probably because he was male. Yes, that had a lot to do with it, she had to admit. He fancied *himself*, which would have been a turn-off even if she had been interested in him. But she wasn't interested, she only wished he would believe that.

'Good morning, dark Ruth.' That had been his opening line when he'd walked through the door at two minutes past nine today. As always, he had perched himself on her desk for a moment and given her what he clearly thought was a winning smile. It probably was to other women, but Ruth found him immature and too ... too effusive or something. She could well understand why he was such a good salesman. He had the gift of the gab combined with a boyish charm. At least, that's how it struck her, in spite of his being six years her senior.

'Good morning, Rory.' She had grinned at him because she simply couldn't help it. He was beginning to amuse her.

'Aha!' he laughed, leaning closer to her. 'Not only do I get the most beautiful smile when I walk in——'

'Everybody gets one of those,' she interrupted. 'I'm the receptionist, remember? I smile at you out of a sense of duty, Rory, so don't read anything into it.'

He ignored that completely. 'I've also managed to make you laugh, at last.'

'No, you haven't.'

'Yes, I have. Well, almost! You nearly giggled.'

She did giggle at that. The nice thing was that she felt uninhibited with him, as she did with Dinah. She could be herself with the younger of these siblings—whereas with Blake Marsden she felt self-conscious, edgy and insecure. Though she had hardly spoken to the man since that first day, she felt curiously nervous every time he walked through reception or came out to greet someone.

Millie had breezed in at that point, looking a little flustered and pink in the cheeks. 'Curses on all garage mechanics! Didn't I have my car serviced only last week? And would it start this morning?'

'We don't know, Millie, would it?' Rory grinned at her and she stuck her nose in the air.

'Take no notice of him, Ruth, he's kissed the Blarney more than once.' She walked straight through reception, her eyes twinkling.

'To be sure,' Ruth teased, but Millie had gone.

'Now where were we?' Suddenly there was a hand under her chin and her head was being turned back to Rory. 'So you're going to have lunch with me today, mm? We can——'

'No, she's not going to have lunch with you today.' Blake's voice cut across that of his brother, causing Ruth to jump visibly. She turned to look at him. He was always at work long before anyone else. He always left long after anyone else, too, according to Millie, though Millie herself always left on time.

He'd gone on, addressing his brother but looking directly at Ruth. 'We'll be having a working lunch today—you, me and Di. In the meantime I'd like to have a word with you in my office now.' He shifted his

outsized frame from the doorway leading to the
corridor, effectively telling his brother to go through
straight away.

Rory did so, winking cheekily at Ruth as he slid his
behind from her desk. 'Some other time, perhaps.'

She glanced after him helplessly, feeling trapped in
the look of displeasure on the older man's face. 'Have
you nothing to do?' Blake demanded.

'Yes, I—I've got lots to do. I was——'

'Then I suggest you get on with it,' he snapped,
'instead of flirting with someone who's all too
susceptible!'

Her hands were still trembling at the memory of
that scene. It had happened almost an hour ago but
she was still fuming. It was so unfair! *She* hadn't been
doing the flirting. 'I don't think I can stand it,' she
muttered to herself. It was so blatantly obvious the
man disliked her—and they both knew why.

Granted, he hadn't fired her. He didn't feel there
were grounds for that, quite rightly. But she had made
such a bad impression on him that day she'd almost
walked under his car, it was as though he couldn't rid
himself of that impression. He'd called her a stupid
woman then. Did he still think of her as such?

His attitude was unbearable but . . . but she had to
calm down. Give it, him, a fair trial. Maybe he was
still suffering from jet-lag? Millie had said he'd be
'normal' by Friday. Was he? Was he always so
aggressive?

When she left the building that night, Ruth decided
the answer to that question was yes. It was seeing his
car that made up her mind. She paused to look at it
from all angles, pillar-box red, low-slung, powerful. It
was a Jaguar XJ12 and it suited him. It was an
aggressive sort of car if ever she'd seen one.

CHAPTER FIVE

'THEN why don't you leave? Hand your notice in tomorrow if you're unhappy.'

Ruth and Wendy were in the living-room. Derek hadn't got back from London yet. Ruth had got home later than usual, too, she'd stayed behind to finish a job Millie had been doing. Millie never worked overtime; she couldn't, she had a husband and two children to look after. 'It's—I'm not. Not exactly. I get on so well with everyone, especially Dinah. It's just *him*, his attitude towards me. Honestly, Wendy, it's as though Millie and I see two different men. She thinks the world of him. I often hear laughter coming from his office, hers and his, when she's in with him. But with me, there's—oh, I don't know. There's never a single word of conversation which doesn't relate to work. We don't even pass comments about the weather!'

'So leave,' Wendy said again.

'Wendy, I'm moving in to my new flat this Saturday, I've got enough to worry about without looking for another job just now. I'll give it a little longer.' She held up her hands, waving them about, showing far more emotion than was usual for her. 'You see—oh, it's hard to explain! The devil of it is that just when I think I can't take any more of him, he says something nice.'

'Like what?'

'Like . . . "there's nothing wrong with your spelling, is there, Ruth? I haven't caught you out once so far." Do you see what I mean?'

Wendy did not. 'You take that as a compliment, do you? He's just a good psychologist, that's all. He's aware that a bit of praise makes people work harder.'

Ruth thought about that. Was Blake Marsden devious as well as everything else? No, she thought not. He was far too blunt to be devious. 'It's hard to explain,' she repeated, aware she was failing to give Wendy an accurate description of the man. 'If only I could clear the air, start afresh with him.'

'Have you tried to?'

'Impossible! Wendy, haven't you been listening to me? I've told you, the man's unapproachable!'

'Dear me! He's really got under your skin, hasn't he? What's he like? Sssh! Calm down! Of course I've been listening. I mean what's he like physically?'

'Big.'

'I know that much. You've told me you feel petite standing next to him, so he must be tall!' Wendy started laughing but she sobered quickly at Ruth's next words.

'He's handsome, very handsome.'

'Really?' Wendy's eyebrows shot up. 'You've never mentioned that before.'

'It isn't relevant.' Ruth spoke dismissively. What had his looks got to do with anything? She soon realised what Wendy was getting at.

'How old is he?'

'Thirty-four, according to Millie. He looks older.'

'So he's thirty-four, he's very handsome and—and now I get the picture. You fancy him.'

Ruth looked at her sister-in-law in disgust. 'Never in a million years,' she said, putting plenty of space between her words. 'I don't even think that's funny, Wendy.'

'Pardon me.' For the first time ever, there was a momentary awkwardness between them, a sudden silence. It was interrupted by the sound of Derek's footsteps approaching the front door. 'I'm sorry,' Ruth said quickly, sincerely. 'I know I'm a bit touchy lately.'

Wendy smiled warmly. 'Forget it. You've had a lot to put up with these past few months.'

'I'm still not over Garry, I suppose.' The younger woman spoke quietly, knowing this was something of an admission even to herself.

Wendy didn't answer that. She got up to greet her husband.

Saturday was chaotic. Ruth had no idea how she would have coped, moving into her flat, without Derek and Wendy's help. They were marvellous. The problem was that the previous owners were moving out and Ruth was moving in, all on the same day.

The department store from which she had ordered a bed, a three-piece suite and various other items, delivered too early. Their van rolled up during the morning instead of the afternoon, as promised. Consequently, it had to be offloaded into Ruth's garage, which went with the flat. And, needless to say, the removal men who were emptying the flat for the previous owners could not stick around to give a hand. Wendy was not allowed to lift anything heavy— which left Ruth and Derek to do the shifting.

'Impossible!' Derek surveyed the tall and slender form of his sister, noticing for the first time that she had lost quite a bit of weight. 'Had the flat been on the ground floor, we might have coped. But there's no way you're going to be able to help me up a flight of stairs with that lot. No, we'll go home and I'll get Roger from next door. He'll help, don't worry.'

Ruth tried not to and failed. She was only too grateful that the carpets were in. She'd bought them off the previous owners and they weren't half bad; they were self-coloured, a sort of greyish-pink, throughout the flat. Except for the kitchen. In there, there were red and white checked tiles on the floor. She liked those, she had plans for making gingham curtains to cheer the room up even more. As soon as she got her sewing-machine from her parents' house, she'd get down to that task and a few others.

She wasn't going back to Wolverhampton to visit, not yet. Her parents were driving down next week-end instead. They wanted to see her new home, naturally, and they were bringing everything Ruth had asked them to bring. Tabatha, of course, was top of her list.

On Monday morning Ruth went in to Dinah's office, sat heavily on a chair and shook her head wearily. 'Good morning, Dinah. I am now the proud owner of one one-bedroomed flat. It occurs to me I should give you my new address for the records.'

'How did it go?'

'It went.' Ruth sighed. 'My back is killing me. If I moved the furniture around once yesterday, I did it ten times. Trying to settle things just where I want them. You must know what it's like.' She went on to describe the bad timing as far as deliveries and removals were concerned.

'Oh, I know, I know,' her boss sympathised. 'I've had my share of that. Mind you, moving out of the matrimonial home was the worst. I'll never forget that pantomime——'

'Matrimonial?' Ruth interrupted. She couldn't stop herself. It had never occurred to her that Dinah had been married. 'You've been married?'

'Yes.' Dinah smiled but it didn't reach her eyes. And her voice was overly-casual. 'Tried it once, didn't like it. The same goes for Rory.'

'Rory's been married?' Millie had never mentioned any of this!

'He tried it once, he didn't like it, either.' Dinah was keeping this very light, so much so that Ruth knew she shouldn't ask any more. But ... 'And what about Blake? Did he——'

'No, no, no. No fear of that! Our Blake doesn't have time for such—frivolities.'

It was more than enough to shut Ruth up. What did it mean? Did Blake Marsden think of marriage as something—*frivolous*? She asked Millie about that when they happened to coincide in the ladies' room mid-morning. She couldn't help herself. 'What did Dinah mean, Millie? Have you any idea?'

'Bless you, I don't think there's anything complicated about it. In fact I know there isn't.' She pulled a face at herself in the mirror, dragged a comb carelessly through her blonde curls. 'I'll have to have this trimmed. That lousy perm I had ... would you look at it? It's beginning to look like cotton wool.'

Ruth said nothing. She took out her lipstick and did a quick repair job. Was this Millie's way of telling her not to be nosy?

That wasn't the case. The absence of a comment from Ruth about her hair made Millie look at her. 'Ruth? Sorry, I wasn't fobbing you off, if that's what you're thinking. No, it's simply that himself hasn't got time for marriage. He has his fair share of women when the mood takes him, but marriage, no! Haven't you noticed he's married to his business?'

Alone, Ruth looked at herself in the mirror, wondering why she was frowning so.

It was precisely that which caused the next bit of trouble between her and Blake. Her frowning. Not that she was aware of what she was doing. At first she had no idea what the man was talking about.

It was almost two weeks after she'd moved into her flat, on a Friday morning. It was mid-July, there had been three days of solid sunshine but today the English summer was doing one of its typical tricks. It was raining so hard, it was almost dark outside. Blake had gone out just after nine and he came back at eleven, his thick, jet-black hair clinging wetly against his skull, accentuating the carved lines of his face so that his features looked vaguely demonic.

Scowling, he shook himself as he came through the doors, shuffling his feet against the door mat in an effort to dry them a little. 'Ruth, do you think you could find it in your heart, just once, to take that wretched frown off your face when you look at me?'

'Pardon?' She hadn't the faintest idea what he meant.

'I said—dammit, never mind.' He strode over to her desk. 'You're doing it again!' He bent down, supporting himself on one arm as he leaned unnecessarily close to her, so close that she could see her own reflection in the depths of his eyes. 'Can't you smile occasionally? What I'm saying is if you greet our buyers the way you greet me every day, I'll be bankrupt within a year!'

Then he was gone, swinging himself and his briefcase through the doors before she could even think of an answer, much less voice one.

Tears welled up in her eyes. She reached for a sheet of plain paper. She was going to type out her resignation right now and take it in to Dinah. What was the *matter* with the man? Why did he have such an obnoxious attitude towards her? God, how she wanted to give him a piece of her mind. And this was so unlike her, so unlike her!

She never got round to typing her resignation. Suddenly she was bombarded with telephone calls. The switchboard did go mad from time to time, especially on Fridays, for some reason. Then Dinah was by her side, getting pleasantly frantic because she'd misplaced a file. Ruth found it for her and Dinah's gratitude almost made up for Blake's aggression. Almost.

Someone called to fix the coffee machine which was in the rest-room where the staff took their lunch on days when it wasn't fit to go out. Ruth normally took sandwiches to work and ate them with two of the women from accounts. The factory had its own rest-room and limited cooking facilities. Today, all thoughts of lunch went out of her mind; she wasn't hungry, she was seething behind her calm façade. Next, the photocopying machine broke down and it was left to her to call the mechanic. Blake gave her a long list of people he wanted her to get on the phone for him, a call came from the school Millie's children went to, and shortly afterwards Millie left for the day because one of her twins had been taken ill. At three in the afternoon, Dinah called her in to take dictation and at four o'clock, Blake summoned her.

'I have to go out for a while,' he informed her. 'I'll be in the factory, in the cutting-room with Tommy. So keep my calls at bay.' He didn't even look up, was scribbling on a notepad. 'It's unfortunate Millie's had to take off—I trust you can cope with this. I want it finished today. You won't mind working a little late, if necessary?'

Ruth stood, looking down at the dark head. His hair was blacker than hers, so dark it was almost blue-black. He needed a haircut. It was straight and thick and normally quite neat but it looked untamed right now. Maybe that was due to the soaking he'd had earlier. Thankfully, the rain had stopped after lunch-time.

All these thoughts went through her mind as he spoke. She also caught herself thinking that he really was a very attractive man physically, that it was a great shame he had a hateful personality. Detachedly, she thought all of this. Wordlessly, she picked up the cassette he slid across the desk. Her anger from the morning's episode had faded but there was still that nervousness inside her, that inexplicable something which always happened when she was in the same room with him.

She wasn't going to say anything. She could and she would rise above the temptation to retort. She never minded working late if necessary, he should have known that by now.

She was at the door when he spoke. 'Cat got your tongue, Ruth?'

She turned, overcome by a sudden sadness. But she wasn't going to let him see it, she didn't want him to know how easily he could hurt and upset her. She was too sensitive, everyone told her that. People had always told her that.

So she smiled instead. Deliberately, bravely, she gave him the smile he had earlier criticised her for never giving to him.

And how did he reward her? With a twist of that mean mouth of his, that's how. A scowl and a half-bored, 'Oh, for God's sake!'

Happily, Ruth didn't see him for some time after that. He was off the premises for quite a while.

She was there in reception when he came back. The offices were as quiet as the grave. It was six-fifty and everyone else had left long since. Having finished Dinah's work before she left for the week-end, Ruth had then set about Blake's. Thanks to the ear-phones she was wearing and the clicking of her typewriter keys, she didn't hear him come in. Having been in the factory, at the rear, he came in through the back entrance and her first awareness that anyone was there was when she felt someone tap her shoulder.

She almost jumped out of her skin. Alarmed, she spun her typing-chair round so quickly that her feet collided with his. He was standing right next to her. 'My, my,' he drawled. 'Aren't you the nervous one?'

'You gave me a scare!'

'So I see. Is that door locked?'

Her eyes moved to the outer reception door. 'No. Why should it be?'

'Because you've been alone in here, that's why,' he said impatiently. 'Because anyone could walk in! I've told you about this before.'

Had he? She couldn't recall whether he had or not. She shrugged. 'Well, I'm still in one piece. Nothing happened.'

'That doesn't make it . . . oh, what's the use?' He shook his head, running a hand tiredly through his hair, hair which was wet again. 'Talking to you is like trying to swim through semolina.'

Talking to you is equally impossible, she answered silently. She averted her eyes. She kept them firmly on a big panda sitting on a shelf on the wall. It was looking at her with a doleful expression, as if to apologise for Blake's behaviour. 'I'm on the last letter,' she said crisply, still not looking at him. 'I've put the others on your desk for signing. I've stamped the envelopes so we can get them off tonight.' They normally used a franking machine but that necessitated handing the mail in at a post office, and it was too late for that.

'Okay, I'll see to them. Let me know when you've finished, I'll give you a lift home. It's pouring again out there.'

A lift home? Not likely! Her eyes moved to the windows, it was ominously dark considering the nights were light but no amount of rain would induce her to get inside a car with him! 'No, thank you,' she said coldly. 'Rain doesn't worry me. I won't melt.'

Blake Marsden stopped in his tracks. He turned slowly, his chest expanding as he took a long, slow breath. He was almost at the end of his tether with this girl. 'I doubt whether a furnace could do that to you, Ruth.' His hand came up, one long finger pointed at her. 'You will wait here for me. I can have you home and dry in less than ten minutes. My God, not only are you stubborn, you really are stupid, aren't you?'

That did it. It was, as they say, the last straw. Ruth put on a spurt and finished the letter in her typewriter. She then took a plain sheet of paper and, this time, she typed out her resignation. She slipped it in an envelope and left it on Dinah's desk. Enough was enough. Her personal life was bad enough, she didn't need this, too! Her nights were lonely and her days were a misery. Well, not for much longer!

She didn't take his last letter in to him. She left it on her desk, where he couldn't miss it on his way out.

Pulling on her jacket, wishing it were a raincoat, she opened the doors quietly and slipped out of the building. If only she'd accepted Derek and Wendy's offer of her going on holiday with them! They were leaving for Spain in the morning and would be away for three weeks. What an idiot she was, she'd thought it too soon to take a long break from her new job, so she'd refused. What irony!

The walk from the estate to the bus-stop was several hundred yards and she was soaked before she'd covered fifty. By the time she was standing at the bus-stop, the rain was dripping from her clothes. She didn't even have a rain hood with her; when she'd left the flat early that morning, there had been no sign of rain, it had set in after she'd got to work.

The minutes ticked by as she waited, shivering even though it wasn't cold. Trucks drove past, cars drove past and three buses came in a row. None of them were hers. It would have been quicker to walk, she realised too late. Someone in a white Ford slowed to a halt and offered her a lift. Not bothering even to answer, she averted her head.

Then another car came to a halt, a car she couldn't fail to recognise. There was the hum of an electric window and Blake's voice. 'Changed your mind about that lift?'

'No, I haven't.'

'Get in, Ruth.'

'No, thank you.'

'Damn you, woman,' he bellowed. 'Get in this car or I'll come round there and throw you in!'

A bastard, he might be, she reasoned imperturbably, but he wouldn't do that.

She was wrong.

He didn't move quickly. He got out of the car and walked round to her almost lazily. He clamped his hand around her forearm so hard that she yelped. 'You're hurting me!' She tried to pull away from him, her long, wet hair flying across her face as she tried to jerk away—to no avail.

With his free hand he caught hold of her hair and pulled it slowly towards him until her face was only inches from him, just about in line with his throat. 'Isn't this where we came in?' he asked. 'You looked like a drowned rat when I first met you. If I'd known then what I know now, I'd never have gone to Wolverhampton that day!'

'Believe me, I wish——'

'Now get *in*!' He flung the passenger door open, not waiting for co-operation. Oh, no, he carried out his threat to the letter, lifting her bodily and dumping her on the plush leather seat so she was half-sitting, half-lying in the most undignified manner.

He was back behind the wheel before she'd retrieved her skirt; it had ridden up her legs during his man-handling, to reveal a long, slender expanse of thigh—the sight of which he ignored completely. He shoved the car into gear and pulled away with a squeal of tires and a speed which terrified her.

He drove like a maniac, just as she had known he would. Taking the line of least resistance, she said nothing, she kept her eyes closed for most of the time, praying the police would pull him up.

'Okay.' His voice was cold, telling her he would stand no nonsense, no argument. 'Direct me from here. I'm not sure where your flats are.'

'It's Pine Court. Take the first left, second left then first right.'

They were outside the four-storey building in a flash. 'Thank you and good night.' Ruth reached for the door-handle, proud because she had given him no feedback at all. It was the quickest way of getting rid of him, *away* from him.

She was wrong again. He got out of the car, too. 'Which floor are you on?'

She put her hand on her chest, her heart was pounding almost painfully. Never in her life had she felt such a strong emotion; she had certainly never felt such hatred for someone. 'The first. I can manage from here, thank you.'

'I'm coming in with you.'

Her mouth fell open. 'What for?'

They were looking straight at one another now. 'For a cup of coffee. And because I want to talk to you. Yes, in that order, I think.'

He could think what he liked. 'That's out of the question!'

In one swift, easy movement, he caught hold of Ruth's elbows and pulled her roughly against him. 'If you argue with me one more time, I shall make you pay for it with more than the loss of dignity. Now lead the way, I'm getting soaked!'

She honestly had no choice. He was furious with her, his voice shook and his eyes had gone dangerously darker. Forgetting about the chaos her flat was in, about the sewing-machine on the dining-table, the pieces of gingham curtains strewn around, she did as she was told. She did stop at her front door, though, she thought it was worth a try. She took out her key and turned to face him, looking him straight in the eye, determined to keep her composure. 'All right, you've delivered me safely to my door. But I want you to go now. I don't know what you have against me, Blake, but I know your dislike of me is unfounded, that much I do know. So,' she shrugged, 'I've handed in my notice, I've left a letter of resignation on Dinah's desk.' She turned away and pushed her key into the lock. 'That should brighten up your week-end.'

'What the hell are you talking about? What dislike? What do you think I have against you . . . apart from your *attitude*?'

'*My* attitude?' She spun round to face him, her soft brown eyes wide. 'I couldn't pass the time of day with you, without getting scowled at!'

'Supposing you try it some time and find out?'

They were standing in her doorway. Tabatha was brushing against her legs in welcome, meowing loudly, but she didn't even hear her. Her days with Marsdens were over—as good as—and since she had this opportunity of speaking to him in private, she was going to tell him exactly what she thought of him.

The trouble was she started crying halfway through her tirade. She hated this sort of scene, she hated him, she hated her own frustration, her inability to find the right words when she wanted them. Here was her chance, and she was going to take it. She began quite well but the weeks, the months, of tension caught up with her. 'There's nothing wrong with my attitude! It *can't* be me! How can it when I get on with everyone except you? I've never had problems getting on with people—unless there's something radically wrong with them. It's *you*, it's—you pick on me over every little thing. You—you criticise me for not smiling when all I ever get from you are black looks. And I don't know what I've done!'

It was at that point her eyes filled with tears. She sniffed, watching him watching her, his eyes keen, his expression deadly serious. 'Wh-whatever it is, I'm innocent! You even accused me of flirting with your brother.' She went on determinedly, ignoring her tears, ignoring the look of surprise on his face. Her voice had risen so that it was offensive even to her own ears, she knew she sounded like a shrew. But she couldn't help it. She wanted to strike out at him physically instead of fumbling inadequately with words. He was looking at her now as if she'd gone mad. 'Well, damn you, Blake Marsden, I wasn't. Rory was flirting with *me*!'

'Don't you think I know that?' he said quietly, so quietly she knew she'd misheard.

'What?'

'Do you *mind*?' A third voice intervened.

Ruth turned to see the old man who lived opposite and one door down from her. She was only on nodding terms with him. His appearance, the fact that he'd obviously heard what she'd just said, embarrassed her terribly. 'Oh! I——'

'Really,' the man said. 'If you two must have a row, you could at least go indoors to do it!'

'You're absolutely right.' Blake looked at him gravely. 'We do apologise. Don't we, Ruth?'

'Yes, I—yes.' She could feel colour rising in her cheeks. How lovely this was! What would her new neighbours think of her now?

Blake dealt with that. The old man's eyes narrowed suspiciously and he looked from Blake back to the tearful Ruth. 'Are you all right, miss?'

She knew what he was thinking, the old, 'is this man bothering you?' Yes, was the answer to that, but she couldn't say so. 'I'm fine, really. I—we——'

'We were having a lovers' spat,' Blake said smoothly. 'You know how it is. No doubt we'll kiss and make up. Won't we, darling?' And with that he bent his head and brushed his lips lightly over Ruth's.

The old man's door closed at once. Ruth jerked her head away, but Blake caught hold of her chin, his eyes laughing into hers. 'That got rid of him, eh?'

She should have been able to laugh. She should at least have displayed indignation, since that was what she was feeling. Instead she stood stock still except for the hand going unconsciously to brush against her lips. She felt rooted to the spot.

'That bad, was it?' Blake propelled her into motion, steered her indoors. 'Perhaps you'd better go and wash your mouth.'

'Blake ...' She felt dizzy. She'd had nothing to eat since breakfast and it had been a long, hard day. '... stop it. *Please!*'

There was sudden, welcome silence as their eyes met. Even Tabatha kept quiet, she was standing between them, looking up at them.

Blake smiled at her, a genuine, heartwarming smile which made something inside her soften. They had just communicated with one another. Thank Heaven for that! 'I'll make the coffee,' he said.

'No, I'll——'

'Ruth, *I'll* do it. Okay? Let's cool down, all right? You go and do something about your hair. Dry it. You look like something your cat's dragged in.'

There was no sarcasm this time. She couldn't possibly have taken offence this time. He had spoken with a softness she would never have believed him capable of.

Oh, did she look a wreck! When she caught sight of herself in the bathroom mirror, she stripped off at once and stepped into the shower. She was out again in four minutes flat. Years of practice. She'd even shampooed her hair.

Rubbing it dry, she thought of putting on her housecoat and immediately dismissed the idea. Long, unsexy and unrevealing though it was, it would be quite the wrong thing to do. There had been enough misunderstandings between her and Blake Marsden, she didn't want any more. Especially one of that nature.

She slipped into her bedroom, pulled on jeans and a T-shirt and went into the living-room to find him examining the tapes on the curtains she was making.

'Looks like you're pretty handy with a sewing-machine.'

Something had changed between them, somehow. Something wasn't right. Or maybe something was very right. She wasn't sure.

For once she didn't think about what she was saying. She answered him naturally, spontaneously. 'You know what they say—a girl's best friend, and all that.'

He looked up, smiling broadly. 'I thought that was diamonds?'

'Well, I . . .' Dear God, he looked so different when he was smiling. It made her realise how very rarely she'd seen *him* smile, come to think of it. What had she been saying? What—why had the nervousness suddenly come back? 'I—I suppose that depends on the girl.'

Neither of them moved. Blake's eyes slid very slowly over her, over her hair, her face, coming to rest just fleetingly on the curve of her breasts in the soft material of her T-shirt. She flushed, wishing she'd put on a bra, feeling desperately thankful when Tabatha diverted their attention from one another with a loud protest.

'Darling!' Ruth bent and scooped up the cat. 'You must be hungry. I'm so sorry! All this time you've had to wait!'

'That makes me feel just great!' Blake said dryly. 'Cruelty to animals now, is it?'

He had fed her the line and she took full advantage, crooning to the cat as she cuddled her. 'You hear that, darling? It was his fault. He's the reason I'm home so late.'

Blake grunted, moved to an armchair and spread himself comfortably. 'What's its name?'

'Her name, if you don't mind. She's called Tabby.'

He took one look at the cat then looked heavenward. 'How very original! I shouldn't bother with her dinner, she's overweight as it is.'

'That's Mum's fault. I left Tabby with her till I moved in here and Mum overfeeds everyone—cats included.'

'Where did she go wrong with you?'

When her eyes moved swiftly to his, he held up a hand. 'That was a joke, Ruth, a joke. See what I mean? It's your attitude. You've misunderstood me. I'm really a nice sort of chap.'

It was her turn to grunt. She took Tabby into the kitchen, fed her and emerged to find, not surprisingly, that her coffee was cold. 'Sorry about that, Blake. I just had to have a shower.'

He promptly made her some fresh coffee, refusing to allow her to budge from the settee.

'Now then,' he said at length. 'Isn't this civilised? Supposing we sort out our differences. Let's start at the top.'

That was fine by her. She was thinking of the shoplifting thing again. Unfortunately, he didn't know that was what she was thinking about, so when she looked at him earnestly and said, 'I want you to know, I really *am* innocent,' Blake just couldn't stop himself from laughing.

It was a long time before she could see the joke. 'I am,' she said again. 'You've got to believe that or we won't sort anything out! Blake—why are you laughing like that?' His laughter was affecting her, infecting her, even though she didn't know what was causing it. 'Blake!'

He sobered, with an effort. She was looking at him as if she'd never seen him before. Yet she hadn't. Not like this. 'Would you mind telling me what the joke is?'

'Your innocence.' He raised an eyebrow. 'I wonder ... You were wearing an engagement ring the day I first met you.'

Everything was spoiled instantly. He had said absolutely the wrong thing. She'd also realised what kind of innocence he'd been thinking of. She shot to her feet. 'Please go. Now. I don't want you in here a minute longer.'

'He-ey, hey! Did I trespass or did I trespass! Okay, message received and understood. Do sit down.'

She stayed as she was, battling with herself. She had over-reacted and she knew it.

'Ruth, please.'

Sighing, she sank tiredly on to the settee. 'I'm tired, Blake. For heaven's sake, I'm very tired and I'm very hungry.'

'I know,' he said quietly. 'Me, too. Finish your coffee and I'll take you out for a meal.'

Her refusal didn't reach her lips. It flitted across her mind and she dismissed it for two reasons. First she knew he wouldn't take no for an answer and second— well, there was no harm in having a meal with him, she supposed . . .

CHAPTER SIX

'And was there?' Wendy asked. 'Any harm in it?'

'Of course not.' Ruth and her sister-in-law were having coffee in a department store in Ilford. It was August and it was hot.

Wendy, having returned from her holidays only yesterday, was tanned and looking the picture of health. Ruth was a little tanned, too, having grabbed a few hours in the gardens at the black of her flat whenever she could. The weather had been extremely kind this month—so far.

Everything about August had been positive—so far! Ruth had started to take driving lessons again, she had finished her curtains, got the flat almost as she wanted it, apart from some lamps, which she would buy today, and she had decided to enrol for night-school next month.

She still didn't like living on her own, her evenings were still lonely but night-school and the occasional trip to the cinema, a poetry reading or Wendy's was the only way she would fill them this coming winter. She wasn't interested in dating. Two of her neighbours had asked her out, one of whom was divorced and childless, one of whom was single. Her driving instructor had asked her out and ... and so had Rory Marsden. This time he'd asked her not to lunch but to have dinner with him. The situation had been getting out of hand, she'd thought, so she had told Rory very firmly and clearly that she was totally uninterested in men, that it was nothing personal, but that's how it was with her. She did not go into any kind of detail. Why should she?

As for her days, they had improved vastly during the past three weeks and it was this she was in the middle of explaining to Wendy. She had reported every detail of the day she had left her notice on Dinah's desk, the day of the violent rainstorm. 'Anyhow, we drove a few miles and had dinner at an inn, it was a lovely little place. Excellent food.' She recalled how odd they must have looked, she and Blake, Ruth underdressed in jeans and T-shirt, Blake overdressed in a smart grey business suit. 'He asked me to withdraw my notice and at first I said no.' She paused, remembering with some amusement the expression on his face.

'No?' he'd echoed. 'But why not?'

She had been blunt and honest. Behaving totally out of character because she had stood for too much from him, she had not bothered to be tactful, diplomatic or even her usual gentle self. 'Because I don't like you.'

'That's ridiculous,' he said evenly, 'you don't know me.'

'I know enough. I can't work with you, I can't work in that sort of atmosphere. You formed your opinion of me months ago, you've stuck with it. You're biased. It's unfair of you because you just happened to catch me at my worst that day in Wolverhampton, in that store——'

'That again! Have I ever referred to that incident?'

'Well, no, but——'

'Have I ever asked you for an explanation?'

'That's exactly the point. No, you haven't. Perhaps you should have, maybe then you'd stop being suspicious.'

'Suspicious? What are you talking about, Ruth? Suspicious of what?'

'Look, I'd been hauled into that office, in the store, having been accused of shoplifting. You're well aware of that, so don't pretend—the point is, I'm . . .' She had been about to reiterate her innocence. Wisely, she rephrased it. 'I'd had no intention of taking anything without paying for it. And what was all the fuss about? Two birthday cards! Would you believe that?'

'Yes. If you say so, I believe it.' Blake pushed his plate aside, put both elbows on the table and rested his head in his hands. 'You're an ass. Maybe I am, too. We should have had this conversation weeks ago, the day I found you were working for me. Now listen, I'm only going to say this once. I'd been to a wedding that day. I was on my way home during the afternoon, driving through the town centre when this pathetic creature almost walked under my car. I was shaken by the near miss, I bawled at her. She looked at me with big, beautiful brown eyes which seemed not to be registering anything. It was obvious she had a great deal on her mind.

'After she floated away from me I decided I'd get myself a cup of coffee. So I went to the store. Geoff Bell, the Manager, used to be a buyer some years ago, at a different place. He and I did business together when I was doing the job Rory's doing now. That store buys our toys, too, as you probably know. I popped in to see Geoff, say hello, have a coffee with him.

'I slipped out of his office for two minutes, returned to find him gone and you sitting there with a woman who had store detective stamped all over her. Yes, I put two and two together. But, dear lady, contrary to thinking you guilty, I nabbed Geoff in the corridor and explained to him what had happened with you and my car. I told him to take it easy with you because you were obviously walking about in a daze.'

As Ruth related this to Wendy, the other girl reacted with the same horror she had felt on hearing it. 'Oh, Ruth! How awful! I mean——'

'I know. I know. All this time I'd believed Blake held it against me. And it was thanks to *him* I was let off so easily!'

'So—so what happened next?'

Ruth shrugged. 'We talked, thank goodness. Cleared the air. He thought I disliked him because of the way he'd yelled at me and insulted me in the street. I thought he disliked me because he suspected me of being less than honest.'

The two women looked at one another, smiling ruefully. 'So?' Wendy asked.

'So everything's been okay since. Blake asked me again to withdraw my notice, I said yes. Dinah doesn't even know I'd handed it in. He said I was good at my job, admirably adaptable, and that he'd like me to become more involved.' She smiled, checking her watch. They had yet to go to the lighting department. 'I can't really say I have become more involved, just that I'm busy, busy, busy. But at least we're civil to each other now. Harmony reigns.'

Was that all? Wendy wanted to ask. She dared not. She'd had her head bitten off once for implying Ruth might be interested in Blake Marsden. Ruth and men was too touchy a subject. Which was crazy, in Wendy's opinion. Ruth had no more been in love with Garry Anderson than Wendy herself had. Unfortunately, it was going to be a long, long time before Ruth realised that, and it would be no good at all trying to point it out to her.

August moved blazingly, gloriously on. One Monday morning, Ruth got off the bus and walked briskly towards the office. It wasn't yet nine o'clock but

already it was hot and she felt grateful for the breeze.
It was a strong breeze, so strong it swayed the heavily
laden branches of the trees which were part of the
landscaping around the industrial estate, planted in an
effort to soften the sight of office buildings and
factories. It was a fairly successful idea.

She was thinking about the business as she walked.
Blake was the controlling shareholder, the boss, very
much the Managing Director. It was he who looked
after any export sales of the toys they manufactured, it
was he who did the buying and much of the selling of
the executive gifts, none of which were actually made
by his company. That part of the business was
straightforward, profitable, buying and selling.

How had it all started? She had never thought to
ask. Since it was a family business, run by three family
members, had it been handed down to them by their
parents? Had their grandparents started it? She knew
the business was older than the estate on which it was
situated but she didn't know its history.

The wind blew her hair across her face and she
brushed it aside, hardly able to see where she was
walking for a moment. But she hated to have her hair
tied back; it never felt comfortable that way and it
normally behaved itself very well loose, being heavy
and . . . Garry had wanted her to have it cut. He had
told her, in all seriousness, that she would suit
something short and pixie-like. 'Have it done for the
wedding,' he'd said. 'Surprise me when I come back
from Saudi. You'll look gorgeous . . .'

Ruth shook herself mentally. Her thoughts had
certainly taken a turn for the worse. The worst. She
had now reminded herself that Garry would be back in
England at the beginning of October. No doubt with
Angela. Would he marry her in November instead of
marrying Ruth?

She heard the approaching car but she didn't turn to see who it was. She didn't even think about it. Her hair had obscured her vision again, thanks to the breeze, and she was busy clearing it away when the embarassing moment took place. A very embarrassing moment.

The summer dress she was wearing had hardly any weight in it at all; it was one she had run up herself, made from cotton. It wasn't see-through so she wasn't wearing a slip with it, nor was she wearing any tights. Even her undies were the scantiest she possessed.

Blake Marsden observed all of this when the wind caught Ruth's skirt and lifted it waist high—where it stayed for several seconds while she frantically pushed simultaneously at her hair and at the billowing cotton—both of which refused to lie still.

'What a lovely start to the day!' He drew to a crawl beside her, grinning from ear to ear. 'I won't offer you a lift. Who knows? The wind might oblige again!'

Scarlet to the roots of her hair, Ruth refused even to look at him. She walked on quickly, keeping both hands clamped firmly against her thighs. When she remembered which pair of panties she was wearing, she wanted to die. They were white and virtually transparent. God, he couldn't have seen much more of her if—if she'd been to bed with him!

'Cat got your tongue, Ruth?'

The powerful red car was crawling along, keeping just a few paces behind her. She didn't even turn her head.

'Fantastic legs!'

'Go away!' She shouted without looking at him, cursing him silently.

'Don't ever let me see you in jeans again, Ruth, it's unfair to mankind.'

'Go *away*!'

'Aw, you don't mean that. Doesn't every woman like to be admired?'

Damn you, she thought as he finally pulled away, his deep, saucy laughter carrying on the wind. I can't make up my mind about you, Blake Marsden. I'm still not sure whether I like you.

But she didn't dislike him. Not any more. He was . . . okay. No more, no less. At least she didn't have to take his flattery seriously. He was no more interested in her than she was in him.

She was surprised, during the late afternoon, when Millie came and said Blake wanted her opinion on something. 'On what?' she asked, but Millie wouldn't say.

The older girl looked weary. 'Sure, it's always like this at this time of the year.'

'Like what?'

'Busy,' Millie said simply.

The factory was working flat out. Orders for Christmas had been taken long since, as long ago as the previous year, in fact. At least, some of them. In the toy business, Ruth had learned, orders were booked a long way in advance where possible but there was still an acceleration during the months leading to Christmas, an acceleration in demand to which no manufacturer could afford not to respond.

She went in to Blake's office to find Dinah and Rory sitting there. Blake was at his desk. Covering half of it and much of the floor was a large array of samples, prototypes of a new range. There were furry dogs on wheels, teddy-bears of all sizes and colours and various combinations of colours; there were snakes and pandas and clowns, rag-dolls, fairy-dolls with wands and a swirl of golden hair; there were bunny rabbits and pyjama cases shaped like same, not to mention a series of foxes and other assorted animals.

Ruth smiled in delight. 'You wanted me, Blake?'

'We were wondering——' Rory began.

His brother cut him off. 'Hang on, Rory, don't say anything. I don't want you to influence her.'

Blake got up. Ruth frowned, he looked tired. Why did he work as hard as he did? Surely he couldn't need more money than he was already making?

'Come with me, Ruth.' As he walked round his desk, he grabbed by the ear a huge teddy which was about four feet tall even with its legs sticking out in a sitting position.

Wordlessly, she followed Blake and the bear he was holding against his chest. They went into the Board Room, which doubled as a showroom when buyers came in. She hadn't the faintest idea what he wanted of her.

He put the bear in the centre of the Board Room table, facing them, pulled out two chairs and gestured for Ruth to sit down.

She sat, looking at Blake, unable to stop herself from grinning. It was the way he'd been carrying the bear, the way he'd placed it on the table . . . 'Well?'

'Don't look at me, look at him.'

Ruth shifted her gaze to the bear, seeing its face properly for the first time. She took an instant dislike to it. 'He's got sly eyes.'

For just two seconds, there was silence. An explosion of laughter followed as Blake threw back his head, roaring. 'Sly eyes! *Sly eyes!*' He was laughing his head off—while Ruth looked at him blankly. 'How right you are! Absolutely spot on! Why couldn't we see that? Sly eyes! Ruth, you're marvellous!' He leaned over, wrapped an arm around her shoulders, pulled her towards him and planted a kiss on her cheek. 'You're a wizard!'

She pulled away from him just a little too fiercely,

realising she was over-reacting again yet unable to stop herself. 'I'm—what's all the fuss about?' She also wanted to laugh. Had the feel of his body not affected her so oddly, she would have. He was still laughing but she—she was thinking about the kiss, such a casual thing but . . . Nor was it the first time he'd kissed her. Not that they had meant anything, these spontaneous gestures, she just wished he wouldn't do things like that. 'Blake?'

'Rory, Dinah and I have been looking at that bear for the past twenty minutes. They think he's adorable but agreed there was something not quite right about him somewhere. I thought it was in the eyes but didn't want to say so, didn't want to influence them. I knew the eyes were wrong but it—I'd never have described them as sly. You're absolutely right.

'Get on the phone to Redway & Son, would you? Ask them to send their rep round tomorrow morning. You and I will go through a suitcase full of eyes, if necessary, until we find the right ones for matey here.' He looked at the bear. 'They're not quite big enough, proportionately, that's part of the problem.'

He stood, looking down at her, the laughter fading from his eyes. 'Ruth, will you have dinner with me tonight?'

'No!'

Her startled reaction brought a frown to his face. Then he was grinning, explaining. 'I want to talk business with you.'

'Oh.'

'Oh,' he mocked. 'So you are free tonight.'

'Actually, no.' She felt idiotic because she'd thought . . . 'Er—I have a driving lesson booked for eight.'

'You can't drive?'

'Yes, I can.' She smiled. 'I just haven't got a licence, that's all.'

Blake was smiling, too. 'A mere detail! All right, I'll tell you what we'll do. I'm assuming your lesson will last an hour? Okay, have your driving instructor drop you at my house. I'll cook dinner for us, something simple, steak and salad. How does that grab you?'

It grabbed her in a mixture of ways. What a curious man he was, sometimes very proper, sometimes improper to the point of being outrageous. Sometimes courteous, sometimes rude. Sometimes funny, intensely serious most of the time.

He seemed to be taking it for granted she'd not only have dinner with him but have dinner at his house. By telling her he wanted to talk business, he'd virtually given her no option. There again, in doing so he had put to rest any suspicions she might have been forming.

'Well?'

'I—couldn't we talk here, in the office?'

He looked cross. 'What is it with you? I'm aware I'm not your favourite person but you're anti-men altogether. Why?'

Ruth's eyes narrowed. 'Where've you got that idea from?'

'My little brother, of course. He thinks you're the sexiest female since Marilyn Monroe—or haven't you noticed?'

'I've noticed,' she said, looking away. 'And I've told him——' She broke off. 'But you know what I told him.'

'Quite. What I don't know is why. It isn't only that you're not attracted to Rory, it's the kind of life you lead.'

'What do you know about the kind——'

'Look, never once have you refused to work late. Whenever I've asked, you've been willing—and able. Never an excuse, a mention of a date that night.

Everyone's curious about you, Ruth. Millie's mentioned to me she thinks its odd you seem to be sitting with your sewing-machine night after night.'

'It's none of her business. Or yours.'

'True,' he agreed. 'But people are bound to speculate. Why don't you put an end to that speculation? I don't like gossip in the office, so I won't tell them what I know. I haven't even told my brother.'

Alarmed, she got to her feet. 'And what is it you know that nobody else does?'

'That you used to wear an engagement ring. Obviously something drastic happened. I can guess when it happened but not why or how. What did the man do that you broke off your engagement to him?'

She almost smiled at that. How interesting he should be thinking that way. 'I didn't,' she said dully. 'He broke it off.'

There was a brief silence. Blake's deep blue eyes held hers. She didn't break the contact, she held the gaze, unconsciously lifting her head a little. 'I see,' he said quietly. More slowly, he said it again. 'I see. And you're still in love with him.'

It was a statement, not a question. Unsure how to answer, Ruth looked away. But she didn't need to answer. 'I'll see you around nine tonight, then,' Blake went on. 'I'll give you my address later.'

Gratitude was her main feeling at that point. She had given an inch, he wasn't going to try for a yard, he wasn't going to ask more questions of her. And he was right, of course people must be speculating about her. So she would let it be known she was off men. She would mention she had once been engaged and it had turned sour. That's all she would need to say. She nodded. 'Around nine.'

* * *

Blake's house took Ruth completely by surprise. Because he was a bachelor, she had never imagined he would live in such a big place. Dinah and Rory both lived in flats, both in the same block, a few miles away.

She was even more surprised when she saw the interior of his house. Wearing faded denims and an open-necked shirt, he greeted her with a smile and led her into a big, square hall whose walls were covered with paintings, some familiar, some unfamiliar to her. The familiar ones were copies, the unfamiliar ones were originals. Ruth knew this because she paused to look at them.

'Are you interested in painting, Ruth?'

'In paintings, yes, I like them. I love that one.' She stepped closer to the one she'd pointed at. 'Blake! It's—you did it!'

He shrugged. 'It's a hobby of mine.'

'A hobby? It's brilliant!'

He sighed, slowly, an odd expression flitting across his face. 'No, it isn't brilliant. It's—passable. I'm quite pleased with it. It's yours if you'd like it.'

'I——' What could she say? Her reaction had been honest and spontaneous. His offer had been likewise. She looked at him. She took a long, almost cautious look at this man who obviously had a great deal of talent. Talent she had never suspected. She pulled herself together quickly, realising he was waiting for a response. Hastily she said, 'Thank you, Blake, I would like it.'

He seemed pleased, but it wasn't for the obvious reason. 'How very refreshing,' he said, 'to have a straightforward answer to a straightforward offer. No "Oh, really, I couldn't possibly!" You're full of surprises, Ruth, do you know that?'

'I—was just thinking the same thing about you,' she admitted.

It was to be an evening of surprises, it seemed. A moment later a door from the interior opened and an attractive, long-legged blonde emerged.

'Hi!' The young woman flashed a smile at Ruth, put a hand on Blake's shoulder and told him, 'I'll see you at the week-end, lover. If you like, that is. Ring me if you want otherwise.'

She let herself out without another word, another look at either of them.

'My current model,' Blake explained, grinning at the look on Ruth's face.

'Model?' She queried, unable to help herself because she knew with absolute certainty that the girl was more than that to Blake. How she knew, she couldn't say. She just did. And it confused her. How nonchalant the blonde had been! But why not? Blake must have said he was having his secretary—his second secretary—to dinner. Obviously the girl had not felt threatened in any way.

'Artist's model, mistress, we have a very flexible relationship.' He said this with such unemotional frankness, it left Ruth staring at him. 'What's the matter?' he asked, clearly having no idea why she was shocked.

Why should she be shocked? He was a handsome, virile man, a bachelor. No, actually it wasn't that, it was just that he'd been so—so blunt. So had the girl, come to think of it. She hadn't said much but she'd said it all.

'Nothing's the matter. It's just ... I hope you explained that I'm an employee of yours.'

'No. Should I have?'

'But——'

'Relax, will you? Chrissy won't worry about you or why you're here. She and I—well, let's say it was nice while it lasted.'

'It's—over?'

'As good as. We both know it. Now come on, let me show you around.'

The downstairs of Blake's house was orderly and very masculine in an elegant sort of way, his furniture large and comfy and tending towards the traditional, the walls plain and covered with paintings and prints.

Upstairs was different again. Two bedrooms had been knocked into one and were now a studio with vast windows which opened on to a balcony. Paints, easels, artist's materials were strewn all over the place and in one corner there was a cutting-table on which there were swatches and some rolls of cloth and a few of Marsden's soft toys.

'Experiments,' he explained, seeing her look of enquiry. 'Tommy and I dream up the toys and their designs. Sometimes the mood takes me here.'

A most unusual man, she thought, a most unusual man!

He showed Ruth everything, the guest-rooms, all three of them, two of which had *en suite* bathrooms. He paused at the door of his own bedroom, his eyes nothing short of challenging as he looked down at her. 'My bedroom, Ruth. Is that of any interest to you?'

'None at all.' That was the truth. She was still thinking about the blonde, too, couldn't help wondering whether Blake's bed was still warm . . .

Trying to assimilate all this new information about her employer, Ruth followed him to the kitchen. There was a formal dining-room, in fact, elegantly furnished as was the rest of the ground floor, but they were going to eat at the breakfast nook in the kitchen.

'Now sit there and be a good girl,' he said authoritatively, pointing to a high stool in a corner.

She turned to see what he was pointing at and no sooner had she done so that she was lifted off her feet and planted firmly on the stool. 'How do you like your steak?'

'I——' Dear Lord, it was happening again! The feel of his hands against her body had made her tongue-tied. 'M-medium. Blake, I . . .'

'Yes?'

'Nothing.'

'Go on, spit it out.'

She thought, fast. How could she ask him not to be so damned familiar? It would sound childish, even prim, since he only ever touched her in the most casual manner. He complimented her in the same way, too, casually. What on earth was the matter with her? She felt on edge, sitting here in this intimate setting, watching him as he prepared their dinner. He was opening a bottle of wine now, reaching for two glasses . . . But it didn't mean anything, any of it; she really must quell the suspicion which kept reasserting itself, she must stop wondering as to his real motive for getting her here. It made her angry, the thought that he might make a pass at her before the evening was through.

She was worrying about all this, yet at the same time she knew it was highly improbable. If a man were setting out to seduce a girl, he didn't let her path cross so casually with that of his current mistress!

Ruth had said nothing. Blake turned to look at her, a knowing look on his face. 'Still on the defensive, aren't you, Ruth? What's up? Afraid I'm going to make a pass at you now I've got you to myself?'

'Don't be ridiculous!' She answered far too quickly, looking away because she was just about the world's worst liar. People always knew if she were lying, it showed on her face.

'Ridiculous, is it?' He had his back to her as he filled the wine glasses but she could hear the amusement in his voice. 'Sounds like the most natural thing in the world to me. However,' he added, turning to face her, 'it isn't going to happen, so why don't you relax? Here, drink this and tell me how your driving's coming along.'

'I thought you wanted to talk about work?'

'After dinner,' he said firmly.

She told him about her driving lesson and, as she found herself relaxing, she went on to tell him about the silly things she'd done during her very early lessons, laughing at herself and enjoying the sound of his laughter.

For an hour or more she was on a very even keel as she and Blake talked easily about nothing in particular. Her ideas of what Blake Marsden was were being added to constantly, it seemed. During the time she had worked for him, with him, his personality had been unfolding before her like sections of a map. It made an interesting picture. Very interesting.

Enjoying herself more than she had in a long time, Ruth listened to his opinions on this and that, sometimes agreeing, sometimes not. He listened to her, too. More than that, he encouraged her to talk. And she did. Before she realised it, she had told him all about her childhood, her brother and sister, her parents, her teenage years.

By the time they had finished a very leisurely dinner and were sitting in the softly lit drawing-room, Ruth's mood had shifted again. It had mellowed; she felt totally at ease with him. For the first time ever, she felt she could be herself with him. It was a nice feeling.

It was only when Blake left the room for a moment that she actually had a chance to take stock, to acknowledge how much she was enjoying his company. Or was it the wine that had made her relax so? She dismissed that as an unkind thought. It was him, Blake. He had been charming and thoughtful tonight, the perfect host. She smiled wryly to herself as she finished the thought: let's face it, he's amazed you tonight! Time and time again!

'Are you ready to go, Ruth? It's time I ran you home by the look of it. You seem ready to fall asleep.'

She looked up in surprise when he came back into the room. 'No, no, I was just—thinking about something.' She was both disappointed and confused at his suggesting it was time to go home. 'I thought you wanted to talk to me about something in particular?'

'So I did!' He laughed, tapping himself on the forehead as he sat down again. 'It'll wait, if you're tired.'

'I'm not.' Without thinking, she told him exactly how she was feeling. 'I'm enjoying myself!'

His slow smile, his look which was somehow meaningful, brought a faint flush to her cheeks. She only hoped he couldn't see it, that the lighting was too poor. She didn't want any new misunderstandings to come between them, not when their relationship had become such a pleasant one. 'So am I,' he said quietly. 'More than I have in a very long time.'

That, she didn't believe! 'To business then.'

'Right. I want you to be absolutely honest with me, otherwise this conversation will be pointless. Do you envisage staying on in the job? I mean, are you enjoying it, interested in it?'

'Very much so. Surely you can tell.'

'It's certainly my impression. Latterly, anyhow,' he added, smiling. 'It's just that you could do better, you know that, I know that. If you commuted to London you could earn quite a bit more than I'm paying you and possibly have an easier working day, certainly you could get more comfort, more prestige, better facilities.'

'In other words, why Marsden's? There are several reasons but let's get the London thing out of the way first. There's no way I'd want to commute, money isn't worth the hassle. Not to me. I think I'd find it terrifying, I know I'd find it exhausting. As for the rest of it, in the past I've worked in a bank and a Building Society—not the most exciting of places. Interesting in their own way but not exciting. Now, my work's varied, I never know from one hour to the next what I'll be doing. I like the coming and going of people, I like using the telephone, I like the people I work with. And I mean all of them,' she added deliberately, a mischievous look in her soft brown eyes, 'now that I've discovered the big boss is really not all that bad.'

Blake did not react. He kept strictly to the point. 'Millie, as you know, has ties. She's a damned good worker and she's loyal. She's been with me quite a number of years, since she was nineteen, in fact. But she's not really——' He broke off abruptly.

Ruth saw his dilemma instantly. He was loyal, too. He didn't want to voice his thoughts about Millie, ones which might sound unkind. So she made it unnecessary for him to say anything else. 'Because of her ties, she's not as flexible as you need her to be.'

The slight bow of his head was her thanks for her tact. 'Exactly. The business has got to the stage where I need someone with me when I travel, when I'm selling, especially. I need someone who's free to do that. How does it sound? In the immediate future, on the selling side, I have a trip to Rome coming up and a two- or three-day stay in London after that. Would you be prepared to assist me, Ruth?'

'Certainly.' There was absolutely no reason why she shouldn't. Besides, she was flattered. What he was omitting to say was that he needed someone who both looked and sounded the part. Millie did not. Even if she were free to travel, she wouldn't be the right assistant for him, efficient though she was.

'I've considered telling Millie to swap offices with you but I don't think it's really necessary, do you?'

'No,' she said honestly. 'Things are working very well as they are. Besides, I'd hate her to feel——'

'Quite.'

Ruth smiled. 'I've been curious about the business, Blake. About when it started, how it started. Was it left to you by your parents?'

His short bark of laughter was unexpected. He got up and headed for the drinks cabinet. 'Can I get you a brandy? Sorry about that, you must be wondering what's so funny. My parents didn't have two ha'pennies to rub together. I see the way your mind's been working—family business and all that. It is, *my* family business. It was mine to begin with, and now both youngsters are in on it.'

It was Ruth's turn to laugh. 'Youngsters? Hardly!'

Blake put her brandy on a table by the armchair she was curled up in, her legs tucked under her. 'That's how I see them, basically. That's how I'll see them until they prove otherwise. They're both——' He paused, looked at her steadily for a second or two and decided he could go ahead. 'I was going to say immature, but that's not quite right. Neither of them is as self-confident as they appear to be, Ruth. They're insecure, emotionally insecure.'

Ruth reacted only with a slight movement of her eyebrows. Diplomacy had to rule. Dinah and Rory were his co-directors and siblings, Ruth was an employee of the company. Intrigued though she was as to his reasons for saying this, she couldn't delve.

She didn't need to, as it turned out. Blake

volunteered, and in doing so he complimented her greatly. He trusted her and that pleased her to an almost ridiculous extent. The conversation developed because she asked, in an effort to move from the subject of Dinah and Rory, whether Blake's parents were still alive.

'My mother walked out when I was twelve. Dinah was nine, Rory was six. Mother's was one of those classic cases one hears about—she went to the corner shop for a loaf, sort of thing, and vanished from the face of the earth.'

Ruth's eyebrows shot up this time. 'It's true,' he assured her without emotion. 'She just vanished. My father said, and I quote, "She always did have ideas above her station, that one. She's probably gone chasing after one of her pipe-dreams." I wasn't sure what a pipe-dream was at the time. I was devastated by her disappearance, Rory was inconsolable. Dinah was the first to recover from the shock.' He shrugged. 'To cut a long story short, from that day on my father proceeded to drink himself to death, for all he'd appeared reasonably unperturbed. He still worked hard and long, as a docker. We lived in Southampton. He managed very well to begin with, when I think about it. He and I brought up the other two between us. But eventually his wages were spent more and more on booze. It took him seven years to kill himself ... My dear Ruth, why do you look as if someone's just slapped your face?'

'But—I thought——' Oh, there were so many reasons!

'What? Come on now, it isn't such a terrible story. I've heard worse, much worse! Let's face it, this is a big, bad, rotten, lousy, cut-throat world.'

Shocked again, to the point where she actually gasped, she stared at him. 'It is?'

His laughter was soft, the slight movement of his

head a concession. 'Well, sometimes, sometimes. Certainly not tonight.' The smile in his eyes was a gentle one, just a little sad, too. 'You're a smart and sensitive lady, Ruth Boyd. I suspect you know me really rather well.'

'No, that's just the point!' She held up her hands, letting him see her confusion. 'I've been totally wrong about you in so many—I mean, I thought you came from a wealthy family. I had no idea you were——'

'Working class? So what's the problem?'

'There isn't one. It's just that I've been so wrong, absolutely. I'd drawn—I'd taken lots of little threads and stitched them up into entirely the wrong picture.'

Blake seemed highly amused. 'Like what, for instance? What threads?'

She found it difficult actually to cite them. 'Well, your accent—all of you—or rather the lack of it. Even your names seem——'

'Ah! We have Mama to thank for those. According to Dad, she thought she'd give us "posh" names!' He grinned. 'Disillusioned, are you?'

She knew he was teasing her but she answered him honestly. 'No, I'm delighted.'

He clearly didn't see why she should be, so she told him. 'You've worked magic, Blake. You've come a long way in a short time.'

'Not so short. I'm thirty-four.' He waved a hand dismissively. 'We'll skip the success story.'

'No! I want to know how you started. Please.'

'Well, the business started with an idea, as does everything in life. Everything starts with an idea, a thought, if only just a doodle on a notepad or an inspiring dream one remembers on waking. I had a very strong desire, need, to make money and make it reasonably quickly. I had a plan, a dream, and I have made part of it come true.

'I wrote down dozens of ideas to start with. You've seen the result. I started by buying cloth, hiring a cutter for a few hours a week. I paid piece-work machinists to put the toys together—Millie's mother was one of them—and then, in a modest way, I started selling my wares.' He shrugged. 'And now I think it's time I took you home.'

'Just a minute, you can't do this to me! You must have been—what—about nineteen when your father died? What were you doing then?'

Ruth regretted her persistence. Though he answered her calmly, she could not mistake the shadow which crossed his face. 'I was in art school.'

She groaned inwardly, cursing herself for an idiot. Blake had been in art school, a very talented man, a gifted artist, but he had a sixteen-year-old sister and a thirteen-year-old brother who had suddenly become orphans. 'There was no other family who could look after the children? You dropped out of school because you had no choice. Or you felt you had no choice.'

He smiled wryly at her amendment. 'Did I have a choice, Ruth? Would you have felt you had?'

'No.'

Silence followed, a companionable one. Neither of them was going to say any more, they knew that. Nor did it seem necessary, to either of them. Ruth got to her feet. 'It's been a lovely evening, Blake. I'm grateful to you.'

He stood, still, just three feet away from her. 'Grateful?'

'I think you know what for.' She turned to pick up her bag. As she turned back, as her eyes met his, her heart seemed to shift inside her breast. Suddenly she couldn't breathe very well. 'Blake . . .' She took one step backwards, just a small step, all it was possible to take.

But it was too late. It was no good at all.

He pulled her to him confidently but gently, with the assurance of a man who was going to please her and to please himself. She did not panic when he brought his mouth down to hers. Nor did she welcome his kiss. She merely accepted it as inevitable. Why this should be, she didn't know.

Blake's kiss changed that. When his mouth took possession of hers, devastatingly, inexorably, then she panicked. She panicked because every nerve, every last inch of her responded in a way she had never felt before, she panicked because her instinct was to get closer to him physically, to get to know more about the feel of his body, just as she had got to know the mind of the man. She panicked because she could not reconcile what was happening to her. Her body wanted to explore him further but her mind told her this must stop, stop now.

She pulled away, finding no resistance from him. But he knew, he knew she hadn't wanted to pull away. 'Blake . . .'

He didn't move. He smiled at the way her hands fluttered in mid-air, he smiled at her confusion. He smiled knowingly but with no trace, no hint of mockery. 'I must take you home,' he said, 'it's very late.'

CHAPTER SEVEN

'I'M fine, Mum, really. My driving test? It's on Tuesday morning. Yes, I'm fairly optimistic. . . . Yes, the job's going very well. It's super. I'm going to Rome in a few weeks, did I tell you?'

Apparently she had, during last week's phone call from her mother. Bless them, one of her parents phoned every Saturday as regularly as clockwork. No matter which one phoned, Ruth always ended up having a chat with both of them. They worried about her, not because she was living on her own, not because she might be lonely but because they thought she was still pining for Garry Anderson. Not that they said as much, of course.

Was she? Pining for Garry? It was difficult to say. There was certainly one level of her life, an emotional level, which was unfulfilled, unsatisfied. But whether Garry's presence would satisfy it, she honestly didn't know. She hadn't even thought about him for a long time.

She'd been thinking a lot about Blake Marsden, though. She'd been disturbed and startled this week to discover how much she missed him when he was away. Not needing her assistance on this occasion, he had gone alone to Scotland last Monday. It had been only five days but . . . but it felt like much longer. It annoyed her, the way she'd missed him, it was bad enough being so . . . so *aware* of him all the time in the office. And now this. It wouldn't do. She knew that.

After talking to her mother, she got on with some ironing. She got through it in no time because her

94

mind was so distracted, it didn't seem like work at all.
No, it wouldn't do. Not in any way, to any degree, did
she want to leave herself open again to any kind of
dependence, any need of any man. She had put a
thick, protective layer around herself in an effort
to——

Words sprang into her mind. The poetry of Herbert
Shipman:

> *Across the gateway of my heart*
> * I wrote 'No thoroughfare',*
> *But love came laughing by, and cried*
> * 'I enter everywhere'.*

She folded up the ironing-board, shaking her head in
an effort to clear it of the half-thoughts she would not
allow to develop. 'Keep a balance on things, Ruth. Be
honest, you haven't missed Blake's aggravating ways,
have you? You haven't missed your share of the
enormous amount of work he dishes out?'

He was a dynamic man, a fast, hard worker whose
output was astonishing. She thought back to the long
conversation she'd had with him. He had a plan, he'd
said, a dream, and he'd made part of it come true.
What was the other part?

She looked at Tabatha. 'If you were a dog, I'd take
you out for a walk. Look, it's a beautiful, late
summer's day.'

But Tabby wasn't a dog. She didn't even turn to
look out of the window.

Ruth made herself a cup of coffee and sat, mentally
listing everything negative she could think of about
Blake, everything she didn't like about him. She told
herself it would be therapeutic, doing this. It wasn't.
It was a very short list.

She took herself off to the park but that didn't help
much, either. Having made Blake's travel arrange-

ments herself, she knew he had flown back on the Shuttle last night. What was he doing now? Was he with the blonde? 'I'll see you at the week-end, lover,' the girl had said. 'Ring me if you want otherwise.'

Had he? Or were they together now, together, perhaps, in that one upstairs room of Blake's house which Ruth had not seen?

A voice in her head asked, 'What if they are? What difference does it make to you?' And, aloud, she answered, 'None, none at all.'

Heading home, she decided to ring Wendy and Derek. She needed company, she ought to busy herself. She was very disappointed to learn that Wendy and Derek were going out to dinner—a special dinner for two.

'Some sort of celebration?' Ruth asked, trying not to let her loneliness, her need, show in her voice.

'It certainly is!' Wendy's laughter tinkled across the line. 'Oh, Ruth, can't you guess? Come on, I'll give you three guesses!'

The younger girl only needed one. 'Wendy! You're pregnant!' She clutched the phone tightly, utterly delighted for both of them. This time, this time it would surely be all right . . .

'Right first time! Oh, Ruth, I'm so excited . . . and scared,' she added. 'But it will be all right now, don't you think?'

'Definitely.'

'Will you come round tomorrow instead? Come early, come for lunch.'

'No, I'll come around five or six. I've got a few jobs to do. There's a dress I've—but never mind that.' What did Wendy want to talk about dressmaking for at a time like this? 'Congratulations! Give Derek my love, and I'll see you tomorrow.'

The dress. It had defeated her. On Sunday morning

Ruth took out the tacking stitches, snipped at it, fiddled with it, tacked the bodice together again—and it still didn't look right. The material had been expensive and she was determined to master it, the pattern which was supposed to be simplicity itself.

When the doorbell rang, she got up from the floor, which was also her cutting-table, shoved her shirt into the waistband of her jeans and headed for her small hallway. 'Blake! I——' She couldn't believe it. What was he doing here? And why was she so very glad that he was? 'I—wasn't expecting you,' she finished unnecessarily. 'Come in, I was just—the room's in a mess, I'm afraid.'

She heard the rumble of his laughter as he followed her into her living-room. He looked so attractive, was it because the blue of his polo-neck sweater brought out the intense blue of his eyes? Or was it because she hadn't seen him for days? Maybe it was both. 'How did your trip go?'

'Successfully. Put the kettle on, lady, I'm gasping for a cup of coffee.'

She looked at him, turning to see that he was kneeling on the floor, inspecting the pieces of material which were the skirt of the dress she was battling with. 'Why are you here?' she blurted, her voice unintentionally curt.

'I've missed you.'

She stiffened slightly, irritated by his flippancy, his flirtatious lie. Couldn't the blonde stay with him for the whole week-end, just Saturday? 'Be serious, Blake.'

'I came to help you with this.' He picked up the bodice of the dress, held it at arms' length and examined it. 'There's something not quite right about this top.'

'You can say that again! It's driving me up the wall.'

'That's why I'm here,' he smiled.

'What? To drive me up the wall?'

'To take you out for a drive. It's a beautiful day and I thought it a very good idea.'

'I'm . . . I'll put the kettle on.' She escaped to the kitchen, feeling delighted and nervy, nervy because she was delighted. Pull yourself together, she told herself as she got cups and saucers out. Why should you feel threatened just because he wants to take you out for a drive? Why feel you shouldn't go? Of course you should go. It's a beautiful day, you shouldn't be indoors.

She emerged to find him scrutinising the instructions on the dress pattern. 'Here's your coffee, Blake. Don't bother your head about that wretched thing. I know when to give up.'

He seemed disappointed, in her. 'Tut, tut, Miss Boyd. You might but I don't. Here, put this on for me. Let me see how it looks.'

Opening her mouth to protest, she changed her mind. Why not? Maybe he could help. She shrugged, heading toward the door with the bodice of the dress. 'Ruth? Where are you going?'

'To put this on.'

'Do you need to leave the room to do that?' He grinned, 'You're not overlooked. Do it here.'

There it was again, the laughing challenge in his eyes. She answered him in his own language—bluntly. 'I'm not wearing a bra.'

'I know,' he said, his eyes moving to her breasts. 'You rarely do. Why worry? I've already seen you as good as naked, or have you forgotten?'

'Excuse me.' She went into her bedroom, wondering what he meant. Then she remembered that breezy morning and the way her skirt has lifted like a parachute.

'You see how it's supposed to look?' She picked up the envelope of the pattern. The skirt part really was easy but the top, well, it had a scooped neck which was supposed to hang in folds . . . 'Casually elegant,' she went on mockingly. 'And I know this is the right sort of material.'

'Slinky and sexy. So it is. Now, hold your arms out. It's all wrong around the bust, for starters.'

Ruth held out her arms, feeling idiotic and self-conscious. She was still wearing her jeans, had not put on a bra because she wouldn't wear one with the dress—if it ever got finished.

Blake seemed determined that it would. While she blushed at the way he was tucking and touching at the material, he concentrated. 'Hold still,' he ordered, 'I'm going to pin a couple of darts in.'

'There are no darts in the pattern——'

'Never mind what the pattern says. Trust me.'

She did and she didn't trust him. Inevitably there was the brush of his fingers against her breasts. She wished she hadn't got into this; she should never have tried the top on for him . . . What did he know about ladies' dresses, anyhow? He might be able to cut out toys and teddies but—'*Ouch!*'

'That was your fault. You keep moving. Ruth, will you stop being so twitchy, keep your arms out and keep still!'

'God, you're a stinker! You've just stuck a pin in me and you don't even apologise!'

He stopped what he was doing to look at her. There was nothing about him which warned her what he was going to do. Almost frowning, he said, 'Keep very, very still. Keep your arms out.' She did, and he promptly put both hands on her face and helped himself to a kiss.

It might have developed into something more than playful if Ruth had kept still. Instead she stepped away from him, squealing as several pins tried to pierce her skin. 'Of all the rotten, crafty, under-handed——'

'What is this?' He threw back his head and laughed. '*Who* is this? This can't be the Ruth I know, that shy, demure, efficient and impeccable secretary who graces my office?'

There wasn't much she could do, physically. She resorted to, 'Shut up! Get me *out* of this thing! I've had enough of playing tailor's dummy.'

'Tailor's dummy?' Blake was still laughing. 'On the contrary, I've never heard you or seen you so lively. What did you have for breakfast, an overdose of ginseng?'

'It was a lovely evening,' Wendy said, though the credit had been all hers. Well, mostly hers. 'I think your Blake Marsden is something else. He's gorgeous, Ruth!'

'Don't get carried away,' she said briskly. She was on the phone in the office, but even if there had been no chance of someone overhearing, she wouldn't have agreed with her sister-in-law. 'Look, I have to go now. Thanks for ringing, Wendy, and thank you very much for last night.'

After their drive, Blake had delivered Ruth to her brother's front door. Derek happened to be in the garden, had come over to the car and been introduced to Blake. Then Wendy came out—and she had invited him to stay to dinner, obviously charmed by him. All four of them had celebrated Wendy's pregnancy and—yes indeed, it had been a lovely evening.

Yesterday had been lovely altogether. She and Blake had finished the dress very successfully between them before going out. She sewing, he supervising. It had been fun, they had shared a lot of laughter. The only thing left to be done was the hem, by hand. She had plenty of time in which to do that, five evenings, to be precise, before the party on Saturday.

Blake's invitation to the party had been a surprise to her. 'There you are!' he'd said triumphantly, holding up the finished dress. 'Hem it, press it and you can wear it for me on Saturday. I'm taking you to a party and this is just the thing.'

'What party?'

'Friends of mine. In Ilford, not far from where I live.' He'd seen the doubt on her face and had overruled it. 'I don't want any arguments, lady, you're coming, and that's the end of the matter.'

So it had been. But she had wanted to ask why he didn't take his blonde with him. Wanted very much to ask that question. Was he still seeing her? What had she meant to him, exactly?

Of course she asked none of these things. She would not be seen to be so interested. She wasn't all that interested, actually.

'Ruth, did Melvyn phone while I was out?' It was Dinah, coming back from an early lunch.

'Yes. He said he'll pick you up at eight tonight, unless you tell him to the contrary.'

'No, eight's fine by me.' Dinah looked pleased. Melvyn Summers had been on the phone quite a lot lately, but then so had several other men. She was dating more than one. 'What time will you be in tomorrow, Ruth?'

'Around eleven, half-past. My test's at nine.' Ruth felt a trickle of apprehension at the very thought of tomorrow morning's driving test. Still, she was determined; if she failed again, she'd try again. And again, if necessary.

It wasn't necessary.

She bounded into reception at eleven-twenty the next day, her big brown eyes positively sparkling with delight. Dinah happened to be in reception and she gave her a hug. 'Well! No need to ask what happened to you this morning! Congratulations! Right, we must celebrate this event. I'll take you out for a sumptuous lunch!'

'I accept!' Ruth was very pleased with herself. 'I must go and tell Blake. See you soon.'

The look of curiosity in Dinah's eyes made Ruth realise just how much enthusiasm she had shown. She couldn't wait to tell Blake of her triumph—and Dinah must think that odd. She would think it even more odd if she knew Ruth had wanted Blake to be the first to hear the good news, not the second. Perhaps it was silly of her.

Blake reacted just as Dinah had, except that he didn't hug her, he kissed her. He kissed her briefly, lightly, on both cheeks. 'I never doubted you for a minute,' he told her. 'Did you think positively, like I told you?' He smiled as she nodded. 'Good girl! I'm taking you out for a slap-up lunch.'

Ruth giggled at that. 'Dinah's beaten you to it. So it'll be a threesome—and *I'm* paying!'

'No. To both suggestions.' He caught hold of her hand and pulled her closer to him. She watched, as he put two fingers under her chin, the amusement fade from his eyes. 'Three's a crowd. I'll buy you dinner instead.'

There was no protest from her this time. This time, she didn't even think of arguing. She merely nodded when he told her he'd pick her up at seven-thirty.

The two women were halfway through their main courses before Ruth asked Dinah whether there were something on her mind. 'Dinah, have you—is there something you want to say to me? Is something wrong?'

They had talked as easily as ever to begin with but

Ruth had begun to sense that there was something more to this invitation from her boss.

Dinah seemed positively uneasy now, unsure whether to speak up or not. 'It's—does anyone else know you're having dinner with Blake tonight?'

Startled, Ruth shook her head. 'You know how he feels about office gossip. But—he's told you, obviously.'

Dinah smiled slightly. 'I am his sister, Ruth,' she said simply. 'He's told me this is by no means your first evening together.'

'And—you disapprove?'

'Heavens, no!' She was taken aback, nearly embarrassed. 'What right have I to have a say in his life, or yours? It's—well, that's the point. I've never worried for Blake. One might as well worry whether the sun's going to drop from the sky. It's you I'm——'

Frowning, Ruth leaned forward slightly. 'What? I honestly don't know what you're getting at.'

With a sigh, Dinah put down her fork. One long, slender hand waved in agitation. 'Don't fall for him, whatever you do. I've seen it happen——'

'Fall for him? Dinah there's no chance of that! Believe me.'

She was subjected to a long, hard look. A concerned look. At length Dinah nodded, satisfied, and picked up her fork. 'Thank goodness for that. You mean what you say, I can tell. You're level-headed, I should have kept that in mind. Besides, you're not over your fiancé yet——' At the changing expression on Ruth's face, she apologised at once. 'Oh, crumbs! I'm sorry. That wasn't very tactful.'

'It's all right——'

'No, it isn't. It was stupid of me.'

There was a brief silence as they ate. 'Dinah, what

did you mean when you began to say you've seen it happen—you know, Blake?'

'Girls.' She shrugged. 'I've seen employees getting interested in him. Mind you, he's never taken anyone out from the office before. I've seen his girlfriends fall for him, even the ones who thought themselves modern and liberated and uninterested in getting heavy.'

'And?'

'And—nothing. Marriage does not fit in with Blake's master plan.'

Ruth had to force herself not to lean closer again. She sat back in her chair, keeping her voice nonchalant and low. They were, after all, in a public place. She smiled, 'Yes, he's mentioned that to me, that he had a dream.'

'Really? You're honoured! Did he tell you about the Greek Island bit? No, I see he didn't. He plans to retire at thirty-five and buy a house on a Greek island.' Dinah's voice changed slightly, became tinged with mockery. 'There, he's going to sun himself, swim, paint and live the life of Riley. He's talked about this for *years*.'

So that's why he worked so hard!' He was stockpiling his money for an early retirement. 'Dinah, I don't think that's—I mean, I think it sounds lovely.'

'And knowing Blake, he'll do it. Just as he plans.'

'And you disapprove?'

Dinah looked apologetic. 'It's awful of me, isn't it? I've just said I have no right to have any say in his life but—the whole thing scares me a bit. Selfishly, I wonder what will happen to the business. He'll sell his shares. Rory and I will have first refusal, of course, but—dear me, it's just that I hate the idea of Blake living permanently abroad. But he will, it's been an obsession with him for a long, long time.'

Ruth was smiling. She had liked Dinah Marsden

from the moment she'd met her. She liked her even more now. 'You'd miss him. You love him very much and you'd miss him.'

'That's about it. The same goes for Rory. Blake has always been our hero, you know. That might sound silly about two mature people but . . .'

As she went on, Ruth was careful to keep an impassive face, not to give away the fact that she knew much of what Dinah was saying. Much, but not all.

Dinah's version of her background was as succinct as Blake's had been but it was related with more emotion. 'By the time I was sixteen, my parents were both dead. We had no money at all. Rory was twelve or thirteen, Blake was nineteen and in art school. Painting was going to be his career. But he dropped out to look after me and Rory. He's an amazing man, Ruth.' She shook her head in admiration. 'He was always the strong one, always the determined one. I was—at eighteen, I married someone wealthy. He was thirty-one years older than I and I married him for his money. He knew it, I knew it and Blake knew it— eventually. I told Blake *after* the event.' She paused, looking troubled, and sipped at her wine. 'It was such a daft thing to do! Running off and getting married like that!'

'How did Blake react?'

Dinah looked heavenward. 'He was furious with me! He knew why I'd done it. I did it because I didn't want to be a liability to him any longer. I had plans of taking Rory to live with me and my husband so Blake could go back to school and run his life the way he'd wanted to. I was eighteen, such big ideas! Needless to say, it didn't work out. Blake said he'd give the marriage six months. It lasted four. I was as miserable as sin. I came out of that marriage a different person— and just as penniless.'

'But you couldn't very well expect——'

'Oh, it was offered.' She smiled, her eyes softening. 'My husband was a decent man. Only now do I realise how decent. He wanted to settle some money on me but Blake wouldn't allow it. He said it would be breaking every law in the book. He meant his book, of course. I was a hard-faced little devil in those days, I'd have accepted. But I let Blake sort it out with my husband.'

Only for a moment did Ruth wonder why she was privy to all this. But her relationship with Dinah had grown to be quite a close one. She knew she was trusted, by Dinah and by Blake. 'What did you do after your marriage broke up?'

'I helped Błake. I've been helping him ever since.'

'And Rory?'

'Rory's is a different story. Blake insisted he went to university. He married after his second year. He married for love,' she added, smiling ruefully. 'But that didn't work out, either.'

There was silence again. Dinah ordered coffee, Ruth mulled over all she'd been told.

'I can't remember how all this started,' Dinah said at length.

'You were warning me off falling for Blake.'

'Oh, yes. But I don't think I need worry for you.'

'No. There's absolutely no need for that.' Ruth said it, she thought she meant it. Yet something somewhere inside her tried to tell her it wasn't the truth, that she should worry. She, herself, should worry. She had to be careful, she had to be very careful indeed in her relationship with Blake. To become emotionally involved with him would be disastrous for her. Such things did not fit in with his plans. Besides, she told herself, they don't fit in with your own plans, either. Oh, she wasn't saying she would never fall in love again, never marry. The idea of marriage had always appealed to her. No, it was just that Blake wasn't the man for her, she had to be cautious, not allow herself to fall under any illusions that he might be. If she even permitted such unrealistic ideas, she'd end up hurt again.

That evening, she kept all this very firmly in mind. Blake took her to a sumptuous, expensive restaurant which was both elegant and intimate. Their table was probably the best one in the room, in a corner, quite private, and they talked over a superb meal, a solitary candle flickering between them. Ruth was dressed in midnight blue, in an expensive dress she'd had a long time but worn very little.

Though the restaurant's atmosphere, the soft, background music was conducive to something quite different, she did her best to hold herself back from Blake in every way. When at one point his hand closed over hers, she withdrew it. She chatted to him lightly, steering the conversation back to the impersonal when on two occasions she sensed he was leading up to the subject of her broken engagement.

'So what made you leave Wolverhampton, Ruth? You never did get round to telling me.'

'I—there are more job opportunities down here. Speaking of which, I got my new passport on Monday, I forgot to tell you. And by the way, Millie suggested we change offices today. I thought, with the suggestion coming from her, it's quite a good idea, actually. I mean, now we're——'

Blake smiled slightly, looking impossibly handsome in the candleglow as its light cast mysterious shadows over the lean features. 'No, we weren't speaking of work. I was asking you why you left your home town. To avoid your fiancé, I suppose? Didn't want to risk bumping into him, was that it? What's his name, by the way?'

'Garry, Garry Anderson.' She answered grudgingly, looking around, casting around for something else to talk about. 'I—it was very sweet of you to ask me out tonight, Blake. This is quite a celebration, more than I deserve for passing a driving test.'

'And what does Garry Anderson do for a living? And how old is he?'

She looked at him levelly, sighing. 'Twenty-five. He's a nurse.'

'A nurse?'

'What's wrong with that?'

'Nothing at all. Take it easy, will you? There's no need to jump down my throat. I'm interested, that's all.'

What was the use? She might as well tell him what had happened, then that would be the end of it. His curiosity about Garry would be satisfied and they needn't speak of him ever again. 'All right, Blake, all right. Garry was working in Saudia Arabia. He was doing it for the money. He was, is, due to come back to England next month. We were saving hard for a house and—and our wedding was all arranged for November. But never mind all that. You really want to know what happened. He'd been away for five months and—and one morning, I got a Dear John letter from him . . . the day I almost walked under your car. He's fallen in love with someone else, someone he's working with out there.'

Blake's dark eyebrows rose slightly. 'Then he wasn't in love with you to begin with.'

'Oh, what does it matter now?' she asked wearily. He was spoiling this lovely evening, getting into this. 'I can't imagine why you're so interested in him.'

'I'm not,' he said, with a curious note in his voice.

'It's your reaction I'm interested in. You're still in love with him.'

Ruth lowered her eyes to the single rose in a crystal glass on the table. Blake was wrong; she wasn't in love with Garry, not any more. In fact, Blake's pronouncement embarrassed her because it prodded her again into asking herself whether she had actually been in love with Garry at all. Ever. It had occurred to her lately that maybe she'd been in love with love, with the idea of it, with the idea of marriage and that nice little house and . . . and all the things she had once wanted. Or thought she wanted.

Things were so different now. Her life was different, she was different. Both Derek and Wendy had remarked on that, they'd said she was much more positive these days, far more assertive than she'd ever been. The idea seemed to please them. Ruth wasn't sure whether it was true; she couldn't see it herself. But even if she was more positive, she was no longer sure what she wanted to do with her life, she had no 'positive' ideas about her future.

Blake noted the silence, the way she'd averted her eyes, the faint tinge of pink on her cheeks. 'Would you like coffee, Ruth? A liqueur?'

She looked up, wondering why there was suddenly a hard edge to his voice. Was she boring him? Would he rather go home than linger over coffee? She answered haltingly, feeling disappointed. 'Y-yes, I would like coffee, if you don't mind. Unless—unless you want to call it a night?'

She was relieved at the amusement which sprang into his eyes. She was not relieved by his words. 'Does that mean you'd rather make coffee at your place?'

Ruth was not sophisticated enough to handle that smoothly. His implication was clear, it was in his eyes, in his voice. 'No!' She blundered on, not knowing how to cope with this blatant flirting. With any other man she'd have found it easy, but not with Blake. Not these days. It disturbed her. 'I simply meant that I'd like coffee here. It—it rounds off a meal nicely, don't you think?'

'Do you really want to know what I'm thinking now?' He reached for her hand, taking it in both of his before she had a chance to pull away.

'No. Blake, please . . .'

'What's the matter, Ruth? Why does it disturb you, the fact that you're physically attracted to me?'

'What? I'm not! I'm——'

'Lying,' he cut in. 'You're lying. And you're not very good at it.' He spoke softly, his deep blue eyes laughing at her. 'Every time I touch you, you tremble a little. Look at you now, desperate to break this contact with me because you like it. No, don't interrupt, don't deny it, admit it, if only to yourself. Admit that you're as attracted to me as I am to you.'

She could do no more than look at him.

'There,' he smiled, 'that wasn't too difficult, was it?'

She flushed. What was he, a mind-reader? Yes, she found him attractive but there was no way she would do something about it. 'I want to go home, Blake. Now. I've changed my mind about coffee.'

'No, you haven't.' Letting go of her hand, he signalled the waiter and ordered. Then he kept his hands to himself—after holding them up in an attitude of innocence. 'Look, no hands. Does that make you feel more comfortable?'

It didn't, because his eyes were caressing her now. They moved slowly, appreciatively, over her face, her hair, telling her how much they liked what they saw. She wasn't aware that she was doing something similar herself, she actually thought she was handling the situation coolly now. She made another attempt to talk about work, about their forthcoming trip to Rome, and, this time, Blake went along with her.

He drove home slowly that night, obviously in no hurry to part company with her even though, at that point, neither of them seemed to have anything to say. Nor did they drive in a comfortable silence. The silence was in itself speaking volumes. Ruth was uncomfortably aware of his nearness. She wanted to reach out a hand and touch the face whose profile was etched against the darkness of the night. The country lanes were deserted, the moon was bright and high, bathing all it looked down on in a silvery light.

She unclasped her hands, realising suddenly how tightly she had been holding them together. When Blake pressed a button on the car radio, she was relieved. She tried to listen to the music but her thoughts were otherwise engaged. With a sense of dismay she realised how very much she wanted him to kiss her. She wanted this so much, she reached for her door handle immediately he brought the car to a halt outside Pine Court. 'Well, I—thank you for a lovely evening, Blake.'

'Not so fast.' He switched off the engine, put a restraining hand on her arm.

'I can let myself out,' she muttered, annoyed by the amusement in his voice. She couldn't look at him. All she wanted to do was get away from him.

'Well, I think that proves my point.'

'What do you mean?' Her head came round swiftly, panic was visible in her eyes. 'It's late, Blake, I—we have to get up for work tomorrow.'

He said nothing. He just smiled and reached for her, taking her in his arms with the ease of one who had held many women, many times. Only momentarily did she stiffen, try to pull away. It was a token gesture which Blake didn't even bother to acknowledge.

He kissed her long and hard. He kissed her endlessly, his mouth shifting now and then to explore her throat, her neck, then returning to her lips to find them eager, parted, wanting more.

Her mind spiralled into nothingness, freeing her from inhibition, from ifs or buts, from thoughts of should or should not. But the touch of Blake's hand upon her breast changed all that. His caress, exquisite and sensuous as it was, shocked her back to reality. Blake was a very physical person, quickly and easily aroused. And so, evidently, was she. At least, with him she was. The tremor of her body was reflected in her voice. 'Don't. Please. I'm . . .' She pulled away, again finding no resistance from him. 'I must go in. It's very late.'

He merely looked at her for a moment, his own arousal apparent in his voice when finally he spoke. There was also just a tinge of annoyance, just the slightest hint. 'So be it. I'll see you to your door.'

CHAPTER EIGHT

'You look beautiful, Ruth. Very, very beautiful.'

Ruth smiled her acknowledgement of Blake's compliment. It was the second time this evening he'd told her that. They had been at the party for about an hour and he seemed unable to take his eyes off her. So did several other men. Her home-made dress absolutely did not look home-made, it looked casually elegant, just as it was supposed to. The material, 'slinky and sexy' as Blake had called it, was scarlet, a colour she knew suited her. She had taken a lot of care with her make-up and her hair was shining beautifully, long and black and loose around her shoulders.

'There's Rory!' she said suddenly. 'You didn't tell me he was coming. Is Dinah coming, too?'

'Not that I know of.' Blake gave his brother a wave from the other side of the room. This was the first few minutes he and Ruth had been alone at the party; until now they'd been chatting to people. The guests were still arriving. Latecomers. It was past eleven o'clock.

'Hi!' Rory came over to them. On his arm he had an attractive redhead who looked at least ten years younger than he. During the introductions (the girl was a stranger to Blake, too) Ruth caught herself wondering why the redhead seemed far too young for Rory. She looked no more than seventeen or eighteen. But Ruth was twelve years Blake's junior and that didn't strike her as odd. 'I'm sorry?' The other girl was saying something to her and she realised she'd been staring rudely.

As she made inane conversation, she became aware

of the amusement in Rory's eyes. Amusement and admiration. Some time later, Blake remarked on it when they were alone again. 'I wish you'd take it easy on my little brother. He can't take his eyes off you. He's watching you right now, over there. It can't be doing much for his partner's ego.'

A trickle of annoyance ran through her. 'Blake, that's very unfair of you. I've done nothing whatever to encourage your brother. Never. I made it plain to him from the start he was wasting his time with me. And would you kindly bear in mind that he's twenty-eight years old? Little brother, indeed!'

Blake grunted. 'And the little dolly he's brought? How old would you guess she is? Fourteen, fifteen?'

'Nineteen or twenty.' Ruth exaggerated in the opposite direction. 'Not that it's any of your business. You're not your brother's keeper.' When he looked at her in surprise she went on. 'Your responsibility to your siblings ended years ago. You've looked after them, you've given them secure jobs for life, a share in your company, it's high time you stopped worrying about them.'

'Who says I worry about them?'

'You said they were both emotionally insecure.' He had said this, and Ruth thought he was right, as it happened. It was probably thanks to their mother's disappearance, their father's untimely death and their subsequent failures at marriage.

'They are.' Blake shrugged. 'But there's nothing I can do about it, not at this stage. I just wonder about them, that's all. The pair of them. They have partner after partner but neither of them seems able to form a serious relationship. I'd like to see them both settled but it doesn't look as though it's going to happen.'

Ruth couldn't help laughing at that. 'What a nerve,

Blake! Marriage is the furthest thing from your own mind, yet you'd inflict it on Dinah and Rory!'

'Inflict?' His brows came together.

'Aren't those the terms you would think in?'

'Not necessarily. And who says it's the last thing on my mind?'

She wasn't going to get into that. 'Everyone. It's universally known that Blake Marsden is not in the marriage market.'

'Is it now?' It was his turn to be amused. 'How very interesting, to learn that other people are doing my thinking for me.'

'Don't be so clever. And while we're on the subject of partner after partner, would you mind telling me why you've brought me here tonight? What happened to the blonde lady I met at your house?' Ruth kept her voice light, though she was very curious for an answer. She had been able to ask the question, at last, without being at all heavy about it, without showing how very curious she was.

It was as though Blake had forgotten. 'What blonde? Oh, yes.' He shrugged. 'I told you, that was as good as over. It is over. I haven't seen her since that night. I was——'

He got not further. Their hostess intercepted, giving them a mild telling off. 'What is this? Having a party all of your own, are you? Not very flattering. Come on, Blake, it's high time you had a dance—with me.'

No sooner had they moved into the middle of the huge drawing-room than Rory was at Ruth's side. 'Would you do me the honour?' he asked formally. 'While Big Brother's not watching?'

Ruth eyed him a little warily. 'I don't think so, Rory. Your partner might not like it.'

'My partner is in the arms of some other man,' He

nodded towards the couples dancing. So she was. Ruth got up and did her duty, feeling grateful they were playing music which didn't lend itself to the type of dancing where people held one another. After ten minutes or so she gave up and motioned to Rory she was going to get a drink.

He followed her into another room, where the bar was. 'What are you drinking?'

He took her aside, away from those who might overhear. 'So why didn't you tell me, Ruth? That this is how it is with you and Blake?'

In spite of herself, she flushed slightly. 'I just happen———'

'You just happen to have been seeing a lot of him these past few weeks. I had no idea, you know, until he told me. I thought you hated him in the early days.'

'I did.'

'And now?'

She sighed, a little impatient with him. Here was a case of wounded male ego, he was probably wondering how she could possibly prefer Blake to him. Fortunately she relented before she said something. Rory was okay basically, very much so. She had to bear in mind that this confident, sometimes cocky veneer of his was covering something quite different. 'There's nothing to it.' She looked straight at him, smiling. 'We like each other's company, that's all. Don't start reading things into it. Blake finished with his last girl, he needed a partner, I needed a night out. So here we are.' Glass in hand, she gestured around the room.

'I see.' That was all Rory said. It was more than enough to tell her he had his own ideas, but Ruth was content to let it go at that. 'If you'll excuse me, I think I'll go and get some food. This is my third drink and I didn't have dinner tonight.'

Rory and the redhead left an hour later. They came over to Ruth and Blake, explaining that they were going to finish off their evening in London, at some club or other. 'Want to come? The night's still young. It isn't one yet.'

Blake looked to Ruth for an opinion. 'No, I haven't got your kind of energy, Rory. I was just about to ask Blake if we might leave, actually.'

Blake watched as the couple took their leave, looking for their hostess and saying good nights. 'Were you?' he asked. 'About to suggest we go?'

'Yes.' She had never been at a party and remained so stone cold sober. For her, it hadn't been the most successful of evenings. She was aware she had been working tonight—working hard at being casual, with Rory, with Blake and . . . and with herself. The truth of the matter was, she was troubled. On the occasions she'd been separated from Blake she had caught herself seeking him out, her eyes going of their own accord in search for him. And when that happened, she had to shake herself mentally, to direct her eyes and her attention elsewhere.

She was becoming altogether too fascinated with him.

Blake slipped an arm around her waist, bringing his lips close to her ear. 'We haven't even danced together, Ruth.'

She looked up at him, feeling a sudden constriction in her chest. His eyes looked beautiful, so blue and— and intense now. A shiver ran through her. 'I—I think I've outgrown this sort of party.'

'Now I wonder what that means?' Blake was watching her carefully. 'I knew there'd be a young crowd here tonight, I thought you'd enjoy that. Haven't you? Or is it that you're wishing you were here with someone else?'

For a moment, she didn't know what he meant. 'No,' she said firmly, realising he could only be referring to Garry.

He searched her eyes, his own narrowing as they probed hers. 'I wonder,' he said at last. 'Come on, let's get out of here.'

But she'd changed her mind. 'No, I don't want to spoil your fun.'

'Fun?' He laughed at that. 'My dear Ruth, *I'm* the one who's outgrown parties. I honestly thought this would be fun for *you*.'

He meant it, too. Ruth didn't doubt that for an instant. He had brought her out tonight not because he needed a partner but because he thought she would enjoy it. He was here for *her*, and the knowledge touched her deeply. Knowing a sudden, incredible tenderness towards him, she slid her arms around his neck and kissed his cheek.

'We-ell,' he said, smiling faintly. 'What brought that on?'

Very seriously, she said, 'Gratitude. I think that was very sweet of you, Blake. So the truth is you didn't want to think of me sitting at home with my cat on a Saturday night.'

'Not unless I was sitting with you.' He was serious now, very. 'But I knew there'd be no chance of that. I needed an excuse to be in your company. I always have. But I'll tell you this much, Ruth, one of these days you're going to meet me halfway. One of these days you're going to ask me to spend time with you, and you'll do it because *you* want *my* company.'

Half-afraid, half-hopeful, she looked at him. No, he wasn't joking, wasn't teasing. He was dead serious. But what did it mean?

She gathered all her courage together and put him to the test. 'How about tomorrow?' she asked. 'It's a pretty miserable business, cooking Sunday lunch for one. Will you join me?'

He looked pleased, extremely pleased. 'Yes,' he said simply. 'Now come on, let's get out of here. I've been longing to kiss you for the past three hours.'

Ruth reached for her bag, glad to break the contact of his eyes. What am I *doing*? she asked herself, excited and alarmed by his words. I'm slipping further and further into ... heaven knows what. But I can't seem to stop myself! He's my boss, and even if he weren't, the whole thing is pointless. He's playing with me, I know it and yet I'm allowing it. Why? Even more alarming, why was *he* behaving like this?

CHAPTER NINE

ROME, the eternal city, was spread before them.

As the aircraft circled the city for the second time, Ruth's excitement pushed aside that which was worrying her. She had never been to Italy before; she had hardly been anywhere. With three children to bring up, her parents had not been able to afford holidays abroad and she had never been out of England until she was nineteen, when she'd taken a holiday in Majorca with some girls from work.

She couldn't wait for the plane to land, couldn't wait for the day which had been reserved for sightseeing. She glanced at Blake; he had told her he was going to show her the sights. His eyes were closed now. She wondered how he could be so blasé about this trip to Rome. But travelling was old hat to him, of course.

For a moment she forgot the sight beneath her, she was thinking only of Blake. He'd travelled all over the world. She wondered about Greece and what it was that attracted him so, enough that he wanted to live there when he retired. If he did plan on retiring at thirty-five, he had only another year to work. Would it be enough for him, she wondered, to live the life he intended to live? It would be a drastic change for him—from the dynamic businessman to the artist at play.

She turned her attention back to the window. At least, she tried to, but she was seeing one thing and thinking about another. Yesterday had been difficult, it had been a mistake. Asking Blake to have Sunday lunch with her for the *second* time had not been a sensible thing to do, though it had begun very successfully with a meal she'd been proud to serve. That had been her excuse. She was a good cook and she'd told herself she was asking Blake to lunch as a way of thanking him because he'd taken her out twice since the first Sunday, though on those occasions she had *not* invited him into her flat afterwards . . .

Yesterday had gone well to begin with. It had been after lunch, when they were going through the contents of her bookshelves, that the trouble had begun. Trouble? It had been inevitable, she supposed. Yes, of course it had been inevitable. Why couldn't she be totally honest with herself, for once?

One minute they'd been laughing, reading aloud from a book of fun poetry she'd been given on her last birthday, the next minute they were in each other's arms. In each other's arms and going too far . . . too far for Ruth. It had been difficult, calling a halt. But she didn't want an affair with Blake, she absolutely did not want that. And, for the first time, his control had slipped. He had done more than resist when she'd tried to free herself from him, he'd told her very plainly what he wanted to do to her, how much he wanted her.

And I want you, she thought now, turning to look at him again. But it doesn't make sense; you're my boss and . . . and that's all you'll ever be to me.

His eyes opened, just as though he knew she was looking at him, silently talking to him. He blinked, smiled a little, shook his head. 'Must have nodded off.' He leaned forward to look out the window. 'Good, we'll be down in a jiff. Get your head together, lady, we've got customs to contend with.'

An hour later they were on their way to their hotel in a big black car which had been waiting for them at the airport, a chauffeur-driven affair sent by one of Blake's customers.

'Oh, Blake, this is gorgeous!' As their luggage was collected by porters, Ruth's eyes were feasting on every detail of the hotel foyer. It was a very old building, its walls adorned with enormous paintings which must have been worth a fortune. She wished she could linger; for the moment all she had was an impression of marble floors and pillars, paintings, twinkling chandeliers and an air of . . . *expensive*!

Their suite of rooms was a mixture of the old and, as subtly as it could be incorporated, the new. In Ruth's room, as no doubt in Blake's, there was a television with in-house video films, a radio and alarm built into the headboard of the double bed and two telephones. Through one of the connecting doors was a modern bathroom, complete with separate shower, and the other door led to the sitting-room which separated her bedroom from Blake's.

He had warned her they would be sharing a suite, so it came as no surprise. It was only practical; it was in the sitting-room they would be showing samples to the buyers who were coming from out of town.

Today, however, they were scheduled to have lunch with the Roman who had sent the car. Ruth started unpacking, calling to Blake, who was in the sitting-room. 'Is there any chance of some coffee?'

'It's on its way.' She heard the smile in his voice. 'Come out here when you're ready, there's something you'll be interested to see.'

It was the view, of course, and very exciting it was. From their vantage-point high in the hotel on Capitoline Hill they could see the top of the Pantheon off to the right, the River Tiber off to the left. It was Ruth's first glimpse of the famous river and she hoped she would have an opportunity actually to walk along its banks.

She did. Three days after their arrival, on the Thursday, Blake took her sightseeing.

It had been a hectic, hard three days, exciting but more demanding than she'd anticipated. At her charming best and looking impeccable, she had written down orders, laughed and joked with people when it was required of her and sat solemnly when that seemed appropriate. It had all depended on the personalities of the people with whom they'd been dealing, all of whom were seen by appointment. She had packed and unpacked the samples, she'd demonstrated wafer-thin calculators and computer games which were designed with the entertainment of 'executives' in mind. She'd ordered endless coffees from room-service, she'd made and taken telephone calls for Blake and she had been by his side each evening when they had gone out to entertain those people who were spending money with them. She hadn't had any time alone with Blake—except when he was in his room and she was in hers! In a nutshell, it had been exhausting!

Nevertheless she was up very nearly on the Thursday, as ordered. 'We can't see everything in one day,' Blake told her over breakfast, 'but we'll do our best!'

They did well. They covered five of the seven hills of Rome and they started with Vatican City and the awe-inspiring spectacle of St Peter's. Standing in the vast, ancient, colonnaded circle which spread before it, Ruth was thrilled; she knew she would always remember this day.

Climbing the Spanish Steps leading down from the Church of the Trinita dei Monti was something else she would never forget. Nor would she forget the

simple white carnation Blake bought from a flower
stall, the way he laughingly pushed it into her hair,
behind her ear.

It was a day of warm September sunshine, of crystal
fountains, churches, obelisks, ancient buildings . . .
and laughter. The Romans, Ruth thought, were a
breed unlike any other. Blake confirmed that they
were indeed, that they were even unlike other Italians.
'They're difficult to get to know. They don't take
easily to foreigners, maybe because their city is
constantly bombarded with them. They keep themselves very much to themselves, generally speaking.
But they have good hearts and a lot of pride—in
themselves and in their city.'

Ah, but they seemed, they *were*, so temperamental!
Never in her life had Ruth seen so much arm-waving,
so many hands moving expressively—this, from
women who stood chatting in doorways, from
shopkeepers or from drivers who opened their car
windows and yelled and waved fists at other drivers.

On the subject of cars, the traffic coursing round the
Colosseum was unlike anything she had ever seen or
even imagined. It made London's Piccadilly Circus
seem quiet by comparison! At the rush hour, cars
stood bumper to bumper, filling the vast, circular road
ten vehicles wide at some points! It looked impossible,
terrifying. She said as much to Blake. 'Just listen to
that lot, just look at them! As one who's only just
passed her driving test, let me tell you, if you'd asked
me to act as chauffeuse here, I'd have been on the next
plane home!'

At seven that evening Ruth took a bath and hoped it
would cure her tired, aching feet. Much of the
sightseeing had been on foot—but it had been worth
it! Indeed, as Blake had said, it was the only way to do
it. He'd also said he was taking her out to dinner

tonight, just the two of them, thankfully. Again thankfully, they had only one more appointment and that was tomorrow afternoon, at the buying offices of a company who owned a chain of stores throughout the major cities of Italy.

So, for the rest of the evening, they could relax. 'No, we're not going somewhere glamorous,' he'd said when she expressed a desire *not* to do so. She was longing to eat a simple dinner, somewhere other than a hotel. It had been good today, not having to entertain or be at her sparkling best. That made for hard work, and, she mused as she eventually got out of the bath, she had learned something about herself during the past few days.

She lay down naked on her bed, almost desperate for an hour's nap, feeling vaguely astonished at her discovery. She had learned that, basically, she was a simple soul at heart. Yes, she was mutable, able to carry out with ease the various jobs, even roles, she'd performed since being in Rome. She could be secretary, assistant sales person, demonstrator, conversationalist, hostess to Blake's host; it had all been different to her, exciting, wonderful. And yet ... and yet she had derived the greatest pleasure from simply strolling hand in hand with him along the banks of the river. There had been no conversation then, just silent contentment for both of them. For her, his gift of a solitary flower had been more precious than all the lunches and dinners which had been not merely lengthy and luxurious affairs but bordering on debauchery. Such things were fine in their place but she wouldn't want to live at that level all the time.

Feeling chilly, she got under the bedclothes and snuggled down, laughing at herself as she drifted off to sleep. Maybe it wasn't such a discovery, after all. Hadn't she always wanted a quiet life? But not *too* quiet ...

'Ruth? Ruth! Wake up, you wretch! I've almost taken the skin off my knuckles, knocking on your door.'

'What? Go away!' She turned over, eyes closed, and thumped her pillow. She had to sleep, she *needed* to, just for an hour . . .

'*Ruth!* I'm starving, you said you'd be ready by eight-thirty. It's almost nine—and look at you!'

'What?'

'Stop saying that! Get *out* of that bed.'

She wanted to laugh, she wanted to tell him she couldn't, couldn't possibly get dressed and go out. She was shattered. 'Oh, Blake, I'm honestly not——' Her eyes came open as she struggled to a sitting position. 'Er—excuse me, what are you doing in my room?'

'Such hauteur!' He stepped away from the bed, planted himself in an armchair and looked at her with mock dismay. 'What do you think? I'm a walking alarm-clock, what else? You and I have a dinner date, remember?'

She tried to focus on him. She was groggy to say the least. But she wasn't so groggy that she forgot her nakedness. She carefully kept the bedclothes over her breasts as she sat up properly. 'Oh, Blake! Would you mind too much if we don't go out? All that walking today—I'm whacked! I mean, really, I can't even make it to the lift!'

Blake couldn't help smiling. God, how beautiful she looked, though she'd probably deny it if he told her so. He'd never yet known a woman who believed she looked good on waking. They always worried about their hair or lack of make-up or—or something totally irrelevant. At least, it was totally irrelevant in Ruth's case. She looked gorgeous, all pink and sleepy and well-scrubbed. Her hair was in wonderful disarray, thick and black and——

'Blake? Why are you looking at me like that? What's wrong? Look, you go out if you want to, but—honestly, I just can't face it. I'd be most happy having soup and sandwiches right *here*!'

He was still smiling. She meant it. Well, it was all right with him. He'd planned on taking her somewhere quiet in any case. 'Okay, I'll organise it.' He got up, turning to look at her as he reached the door. 'But you're not having it all your own way. You're not denying me the pleasure of your company.' He opened the door to the sitting-room and made a bow like a butler. 'Dinner will be served in here, madam, at nine-thirty sharp.' Then, himself again, 'So get out of that bed, lady, shove yourself into some clothes and get yourself *in* here!'

Ruth giggled. She slipped out of bed as soon as he had disappeared, splashed cold water on her face and brushed her hair, which was still slightly damp from washing. She pulled on the jeans she'd worn that day and a soft, lambswool sweater she had not yet worn. It was new, rose pink, and it gave her the hint of colour she needed. That, plus a quick dab of lipstick.

Dinner was perfect, a simple steak, a salad and a bottle of red wine. It was delivered on a trolley by a smiling waiter and she and Blake ate hungrily, almost without conversation. It was after the waiter reappeared, when the debris had been cleared and a tray of coffee had been brought that they recapped on their day. From the bar in the corner of the room, Blake poured two generous brandies, and Ruth settled on an ornate, velvet-covered sofa.

They talked like two old friends to begin with, two people who had shared many hours of pleasure. Maybe things wouldn't have changed, gone wrong, if Ruth's eyelids hadn't started to droop.

'Hey, are you falling asleep on me again?'

'It's nothing personal.' She laughed it off. 'Sorry! But it has been quite a day, you've got to admit.'

'I admit.' Blake crossed over to her. He caught hold of her hands and pulled her to her feet. 'Come on, sleepy head, I'll see you to your door.'

I'll see you to your door. She smiled at the familiarity of the words. She looked up at him laughingly, 'I don't exactly have far to go, do I?'

Blake didn't answer. With a groan, he pulled her into his arms and kissed her without restraint. He kissed her as he never had before, with a hunger which brought her instantly awake, aware. She was aware of every inch of him, of the hardness of his thighs against hers, the pressure of his hand in the small of her back. Then as the kiss deepened, as she responded in spite of herself, his hands moved to her hips, her breasts. 'Blake, let go of me!'

She panicked. It was too fast, too intense, too—too *good*.

'Ruth, I *want* you! Don't you know what you're doing to me?'

She wrenched away from him. It took everything she had to do so. 'I don't want to hear that!'

With a muttered imprecation he turned his back on her. There followed a tense, awful, silence. Ruth was breathing deeply. She sat heavily, trying to stop her hands trembling, trying to compose herself. 'Blake, it's no use . . .'

He turned to face her. It was as if, now he was no longer touching her, he'd been able to regain control. Quietly, he asked, 'How long do you think this can go on?'

'I—don't know what you mean.'

'You're a beautiful woman,' he said detachedly, just as though he were telling her the time. 'And personally I don't see why you should let this thing worry you. We've worked together every day for months and we were attracted from the start. It's *there*, Ruth, why deny it? It's there, nagging away, day after day.'

She couldn't look at him now. It was the truth. She wasn't going to deny it.

'Ruth? Will you please say something? I'm not sure I can go on like this, wanting you the way I do. It won't just go away, no matter how much you ignore it.'

'Then perhaps I'd better leave. Perhaps we should call it a day.'

'Don't be ridiculous!' he snapped.

She closed her eyes. She felt drained. Yes, she wanted him. Now, right now. But Blake was absolutely the wrong man to get involved with. Quite apart from anything else, he happened to be her boss, which would complicate life in the office, to say the least. And she didn't want to leave. She didn't want to leave Mardens ... or Blake. Only today had she realised she loved him. Fool, what a fool she was! She looked at him helplessly. 'I'm not the type who indulges in casual sex,' she said. 'It's just not my style.'

'*Casual?*' He almost laughed. 'You and me? Casual?' Suddenly he was angry. His voice was raised and his eyes were cold with anger. 'I know what ails you, I know what's holding you back, so don't insult my intelligence. You're still in love with Garry, that's your problem. Yes,' he added derisively, 'it's my problem, too! You're in love with him and yet you want me, physically. And why fight it, Ruth? Who knows, if you stop resisting, you might even find you'll forget Mr Anderson!'

Ruth shot to her feet. He was wrong about Garry, dead wrong, but there was no point in telling him so.

It helped, letting him believe she was still in love with Garry. She certainly couldn't tell him the truth, that it was him she loved. It would amuse him no end, it wasn't part of what he had in mind. 'My God, what arrogance! So you're suggesting I have two roles in your life—as personal assistant and mistress!'

· He wasn't in the least perturbed. 'It wouldn't be the strangest situation I've been in. I think I could handle it,' he added, faintly amused.

'Oh, I'll just bet you could! Well, I couldn't. You've read too much into my—reaction to you, Blake. I find you very resistible. Sorry about that. It must be quite a blow to your ego.'

She stormed out of the room with as much drama as she had put into her little speech. She had had to attack him, she'd had to be dramatic, she needed to use anything she had at her disposal to create the smokescreen which would hide her true feelings— anger, Garry, indignation, anything.

Thank God, thank God they were leaving for England tomorrow evening!

CHAPTER TEN

'I'M in love with him, Wendy. I think I've loved him for months but I wouldn't admit it. Now that I have, it gets harder to cope with every day.'

Two weeks had passed since Ruth came back from Rome. Two awful weeks during which Blake had been withdrawn and moody, two weeks during which she had found it more and more difficult to cope with him.

She had longed for this talk with her sister-in-law but last week-end Wendy's parents had been visiting and they'd stayed over for a few days. So there had been no chance of a private talk with Wendy then or during the evenings of this week—until today. It was Friday, Derek had gone out to a residents' association meeting, so Ruth had asked Wendy to come over for a couple of hours. She needed a woman to talk to. She couldn't talk to Dinah, much as she liked her. Dinah was Blake's sister. Nor could she talk to Millie, for similar reasons. Their loyalty would be to Blake, not to her. Besides, she didn't want anyone at work to know what was happening to her.

'Don't laugh, I'm going to tell you something you probably won't believe.' She looked at Wendy levelly. 'I was never in love with Garry. Do you know, I didn't really know him. I mean, I knew more about Blake within the first few weeks than I knew about Garry at all. And to think I was going to marry him!'

Wendy wasn't laughing. She was, simply, relieved. She had known long ago that Ruth wasn't in love with the man who had jilted her; she had known that from her reaction, the way she had lamented the loss of a dream, a house, her plans, *not* the man himself.

But it was very, very different with Blake Marsden. Wendy had known that for some time, too. That Ruth was in love with him, that it was real ... that she would end up with a problem on her hands. Total honesty was called for now, now it was out in the open. She sighed. 'Ruth, it seems to me you have two choices.'

'It seems to me I have none at all. I've thought things over till I'm dizzy with it. I can't leave, Wendy. I—I know it sounds weak but I can't bear the thought of not having him in my life. I'd rather have him moody and strange as he is than not at all.'

'I was going to suggest you leave. I was going to suggest that very firmly but,' she shrugged, 'if you can't you can't. Nor can you go on like this—either of you. Sex, that's the ... how can I put it? It's driving this wedge between you. So, dear heart, why not have an affair with him?'

'You're not serious?' Ruth had not expected this advice.

'I'm very serious. Look, if you have an affair with him, you'll end up leaving the firm. If you don't, you'll end up leaving anyway. He'll either throw you out because he can't stand having you round him so much, or you'll leave when the atmosphere becomes unbearable. Either way, Ruth, he'll never be yours. And, since you're in love with him, you want him, why not have the pleasure?'

'Coldblooded and logical.' Ruth shook her head, 'Undeniable logic.'

Wendy looked at her sympathetically. 'But it doesn't feel right to you, does it? Poor Ruth, so sentimental and sensitive. It isn't what you'd had in mind for your initiation, is it?'

The choice of words brought Ruth's head up sharply. But what was the use? Wendy guessed. 'No, it isn't. You must think me immature and——'

'And I wouldn't change you for the world. But it does make things more difficult for you, the decision, I mean. And, much as I liked Blake when I met him, I don't honestly think he deserves the honour.'

Ruth laughed hollowly. 'I'm sure he'd be very startled. He has no idea ... he's convinced I'm holding back because I'm still in love with Garry.'

Shocked, Wendy said, 'But that's crazy! Why do you let him go on thinking that? You ought to put him straight on that, Ruth. You needn't let him know you're in love with him but I really think you should clear up his misapprehension.'

'I will ... if I decide to go to bed with him.'

There was a shock in store for Ruth when she got to work on Monday. She hadn't reached a decision. Try as she might, she just couldn't conduct her life so coldbloodedly, logic or no. She felt trapped, trapped in a place she wanted to be, a place she knew she ought to get away from.

'Good morning! Nice week-end?'

'Not bad.' She lied cheerfully to Dinah, it had been a rotten week-end, two days during which she'd had a mild but incessant headache.

'Blake's gone away for a couple of weeks. To Greece. He said something about a house he wanted to look at. He had a phone call from someone, apparently, who told him about it just coming on the market.'

'But—but I don't know anything about this!' Only half of Ruth's mind registered Dinah's philosophical shrug, a gesture which said she herself wasn't in the least surprised. 'He never said a word to me!'

'Well, he rang me on Saturday and said he'd got the call Friday night. I'll bet he tried to ring you at home. Maybe you were out.'

'I haven't budged from my flat all week-end.' The despondency in Ruth's voice couldn't be missed.

Dinah leaned her elbows on her desk, unable to keep quiet any longer. She stuck her chin in her hands and looked straight into Ruth's eyes. 'Supposing you tell me what's going on between you two.'

Silence.

'Come on, Ruth. Blake's behaviour has been peculiar since you got back from Rome. And now this. I mean, I know all about his plans but fancy taking off for Greece at this time of the year, when we're frantically busy getting Christmas orders out! It doesn't make sense.'

No, Ruth thought the same. It did seem odd. 'How long did you say he's gone for?'

'Two weeks. It doesn't take two weeks to look at a house, does it?'

'No.'

'And so?'

'Dinah, I—there's nothing to tell.' She regretted the words as soon as she'd said them. Dinah wasn't a stupid person. 'Look, I'm sorry. But you must see that I can't talk to you about Blake.'

'Won't, is more like it.' Dinah took it well, showing no sign of being offended. 'You and Blake both. I can't get any sense out of him, either.'

Ruth was relieved to hear it. This had nothing to do with anyone but her and Blake. 'I'd better press on, Dinah. See you later.'

She went back to her office. She and Millie had swapped offices long since, at Millie's suggestion. Millie was now working in reception and doing about half Blake's work, plus some of Dinah's, which didn't amount to all that much. Between them, Ruth and Millie looked after them both but because of Ruth's deeper involvement in Blake's affairs, it had made sense for her to be in his adjoining office.

Involvement in Blake's affairs? She smiled to herself as she sat down at her desk, a very wry kind of smile. Well, what was done was done. Blake was away. She told herself this was a good thing. Maybe she'd be able to sort herself out while he was gone. Without the daily sight of him, the pain of him, the longing for him, she would surely be able to think more clearly.

She was in precisely the same state of indecision when he came back.

September had become October more than a week ago—and she had been counting the days to Blake's return.

'Hello, Ruth. How are you?' He was already at work by the time she got there, on the Tuesday, two weeks later.

The sight of him was a shock to her. He'd been in the sun, that much was obvious. He looked a little thinner, too, as if he'd been neglecting to eat. Maybe he'd been too busy . . . living the life of Riley? As Dinah had said, it didn't take two weeks to look at a house.

'I'm fine.' She forced herself to sound gay, carefree. 'I believe you've been looking at properties?'

'Just the one. One I've had my eye on for a long time. I bought it.'

'Congratulations.' Then why did he sound . . . what? Vaguely sad? Yes, that was it. She could see it in his eyes now.

They were looking at one another, just looking. Between them there was a gaping silence which neither of them was able to bridge. Ruth wanted to weep. What had happened to them? What had

happened that was making them behave like strangers?
She couldn't stand it, she couldn't stand it any longer.
'Blake, what is it?' She almost pleaded with him.
'What have I done, really? I mean, when you come to
think about it, I——'

'Will you marry me, Ruth?'

It was minutes before she answered. She just stood,
rooted to the spot, her heartbeats thudding in yet
another silence. She stared at him, knowing she hadn't
misheard, wishing she could read what was in his
mind. His face told her nothing, nothing at all. 'I—I
don't, I mean, I can't——'

'A simple yes or no will do.' Closed, his face was
closed, his eyes almost cold as he watched her.

'Why, Blake? What the devil are you talking about,
really?'

'I want you. Doesn't that say it all?'

'Dear God.' She closed her eyes, her hand reaching
out to the filing cabinet for support. This couldn't be
real. She couldn't really be standing in an office at
nine in the morning, getting a proposal of marriage
from the man she loved, a man who didn't even begin
to love her. 'And that's the way to get me, is it?'

His voice was curt. 'I told you, a simple yes or no
will do.'

'I'll give you my answer, Blake. Go to hell!' She
turned on her heel, desperate to get out of there before
she burst into tears. He was a bastard, an out-and-out
bastard! He was playing with her, just as he always
had. He wasn't even serious. He couldn't be! This was
just a way of telling her he wanted her and would pay
some high price for the privilege.

She sought the refuge of the ladies' room, locked
herself in a lavatory and cried. But she didn't cry for
long. Something hardened inside her, hardened
against him. She hated him in that instant. Oh, if only

he knew how he was tampering with her emotions, surely he couldn't have been so matter of fact? Could he?

Yet she couldn't walk out on him. There had been too much between them for her to do that. She went back into his office and told him to take two weeks' notice. 'I'm not walking out, Blake. I know the work situation and I'm not going to leave you in a fix. Just start looking for a replacement as soon as possible, will you?'

And Blake Marsden said nothing, nothing at all.

For days they were like strangers and it was even worse than it had been before he went to Greece. They were polite to each other but they kept their conversations strictly on matters of business. It was, as he too must surely feel, ridiculous. Ridiculous and impossible. The sooner he found someone else, the better. Even if he hadn't, she was leaving in two weeks. She couldn't bear this any longer.

She phoned the agency which had got her the job and told them what was happening. By the following Wednesday Blake had interviewed two prospective secretaries. By Thursday he'd interviewed three—all of whom had been selected first by the agency and then by Dinah. On Friday the phone rang in mid-morning and Ruth picked it up. 'It's for you, Ruth.' Millie was manning the switchboard in reception. 'I mean, it's personal.'

'Thank's Millie, put her through.' Convinced it was Wendy, she didn't expect to hear a male voice.

'Ruth? Ruth, it's me.'

She knew the voice and yet she didn't. It was familiar and unfamiliar. It was seconds before she realised who it was, and even then she couldn't believe it. 'Garry? *Garry!*'

Her eyes went instantly to the door of Blake's office.

It was closed. She lowered her voice a little, aware of the way she'd almost shouted Garry's name. What she wasn't aware of, what she had no way of knowing was that at that precise moment Blake had been about to emerge.

His hand was actually on the doorknob when he heard Ruth's explosion of surprise. He froze. Without compunction he listened and he heard everything she said.

'Garry, I can't believe this! I can't—how did you find me? How did you get this number? ... I see. When did you get back from Saudi? Oh, dear, I'm sorry to hear that.'

The tiredness in Garry's voice was unmistakable. Ruth knew something was wrong. She listened to him; he wasn't saying anything of significance except that he had expected her to hang up on him. She smiled, glad that such a thought had never entered her mind. There was no bitterness in her, none at all. How could there be? Garry himself had saved her from making a ghastly mistake; she reacted to him now as someone she had once cared for, still cared for in a detached, friendly sort of way. No, it had never occurred to her to put the phone down. Garry Anderson could not touch her emotionally, not any more.

'So you're going to live in London, Garry?' She frowned at his next words. 'Well, okay, if it's that important to you. I can easily get to London tomorrow. Where do you want us to meet? Just tell me when and where.'

Immediately she put the phone down, another call came through. A business call. Ruth dealt with it herself, wondering why Garry had insisted on seeing her, what it was he wanted to say that he couldn't say over the phone. Another part of her mind was concerned with Blake. She looked again at the closed door to his office. Even if things had been normal between them, she doubted she would mention tomorrow's rendezvouz in London. What was the point? Her meeting Garry was something Blake could live without knowing about.

In any case, it was academic. Not only were things far from normal between them, he probably wouldn't give two hoots at this stage. There had been moments this week when she had actually felt that he hated her. It was a saddening, sickening thought.

She sat motionless for several minutes, staring at nothing. It was only when a tear splashed on to the back of her hand that she realised she was crying. It was all catching up with her, all the tension, the horror of the atmosphere at work, the hopelessness of her love for Blake. She should go now, if she had any sense. It was nothing short of masochistic to work through another week with him. She told herself it was her basic sense of honour which was making her serve her notice. It was, partly, but mainly it was ... dammit, it was mainly because she was hoping, every minute of every day, that something would give, that Blake would *talk* to her, ask her not to leave.

She rubbed the moisture from the back of her hand, noticing from her watch it was almost noon. Grabbing her handbag, she got up quickly and headed for the ladies' room. Blake had a business lunch today; he'd be leaving any minute and she didn't want to be seen crying.

Having composed herself, tidied her face and her hair, she went back to the office. Blake was there, about to leave by the look of it.

'Ah, there you are.' He glanced at his watch. 'I'd like a word with you in my office.'

He held open his door and Ruth went before him, hoping against hope they'd be able to *communicate*. He was about to ask her to stay, she was sure of it!

Wanting to meet him more than halfway, she smiled as she sat facing him. 'Yes, Blake?'

He did not return the smile. He was looking at her oddly. 'I'm—off to meet John Lendell in a minute. I'll be a couple of hours with him, probably.'

She nodded. She knew all that already. 'You wanted to say something to me?' Why was he watching her so intently? He looked more tense than she had ever seen him. 'Blake, what is it? What *is* it?'

'Nothing.' He snapped out of it, shrugging. 'I just wondered what's been happening in there this morning.' He jerked his head in the direction of her office. 'Are there any messages I should know about before I go? Any phone calls?'

With a sense of relief, Ruth told him about the calls she'd handled herself and gave him two messages, people who wanted him to ring back.

'Is that it, Ruth?'

She nodded, smiling again.

He got up so quickly he startled her. He strode over to the window and kept his back to her, his voice like ice as he told her he wanted her to leave today, now.

'But—but . . .' Unable to believe it, she stared at him. All she could see was his back. 'But you haven't got a replacement yet! I'm—isn't this rather silly, Blake? I'm prepared to stay another week.' And more, much more! Oh, God, she hadn't expected this. She'd walked into his office convinced he'd changed his mind, that he was going to ask her to stay on, not to leave immediately!

But it wasn't silly at all. Blake had his reasons, purely practical ones. 'First, I've got Millie,' he informed her in that cold voice. 'Second I've just asked Dinah to organise a temp until I find someone suitable. And third, I'm going to be out of the office for three days next week. So you see,' he added, finally turning to face her, 'there's absolutely no need for you to stay another week, no point in it. You'll be paid for the week, of course.'

His last remark was an insult, spoken almost patronisingly, as if it mattered to her. She felt stunned. She looked at him as though she'd never seen him before. He really was a stranger. 'Blake, I——'

'You might as well go now. Millie can cope this afternoon.'

Appalled, she got slowly to her feet. He'd turned his back on her again. His meaning had been abundantly clear: I don't want to find you here when I get back from lunch. He didn't even want to look at her now!

She couldn't speak. She looked at the broad shoulders, the back of his head, his thick, jet-black hair, knowing that this was the last time she would have the privilege. This was goodbye. His contempt for her was such that he wouldn't even turn around.

How she managed a dignified exit, she would never know. While some invisible hand squeezed agonisingly at her heart, she said goodbye to Blake in a quiet but steady voice. 'I'm sure you're right. Goodbye, Blake. Good luck with the business and your plans.'

She went directly to Dinah's office, in no danger of crying, in no danger of losing her composure. She was too numb to react, to feel anything. She made brief goodbyes to everyone, gathered her personal belongings from her office and left.

Everyone was bewildered.

She, most of all.

CHAPTER ELEVEN

As she got off the train in London, Ruth had to stop and think what she was doing here. It had been like that for most of the journey. She had sat, unseeing, thinking of Blake. Only when fellow passengers got on or off the train had she snapped back to reality and the recollection that she was on her way to meet Garry.

She looked round dazedly for the Underground sign. The Victoria line, Garry had said, take the Victoria line to Pimlico. She wasn't all that familiar with London, had only a vague idea of the area where Garry's hotel was.

He had been back from Saudi for two weeks, he'd told her, and had travelled from Wolverhampton to London on Thursday to attend an interview on Friday afternoon. She wondered how the interview had gone, why he wanted to live in London. Maybe Angela came from London?

She found her ex-fiancé sitting in the residents' lounge, as arranged, in the modest hotel where he was staying. He shot to his feet as soon as he saw her, his eyes meeting hers uncertainly. He proffered his hand and instantly let it fall again, as if realising the gesture was inappropriate. 'I—Ruth, I'm very grateful to you for coming.'

'No problem.' She sat down on a chair that had seen better days. The hotel, this room, was a little dingy. Still, Garry wouldn't mind that. Decent hotels in London were expensive and he was careful with his money.

'How did the interview go?' she asked. She was

surprised by her own casualness. Garry was looking at
her a little warily, as if he expected her to behave like
the woman scorned at any moment. She found it
vaguely amusing. Seeing him again meant nothing for
her, did not affect her in any way. She had agreed to
meet him because he'd said it was important to him.
And, since he happened to be in London, why not?

'I don't know. I'll have to wait till I hear. I'll
organise a pot of tea for us, shall I?'

'I'd like that.'

The instant he left the room, Ruth's thoughts were
back with Blake. She didn't even feel curious as to
Garry's reasons for asking her here.

It was only when Garry came back that she actually
registered the changes in him. He was tanned, thinner,
looking rather older than his twenty-five years.
'You're thinner but you are looking well. I was sorry
to hear you'd been ill out there.'

He shrugged. 'I'm fine now, it was just a bug,
though it knocked me off my feet for three weeks.
Cigarette, Ruth?'

Startled, she shook her head. He knew very well she
didn't smoke, but she didn't comment. 'So what is it
you want to say to me?'

'Can't you guess?' He didn't meet her eyes.

'I can't begin to.'

'I want to apologise, of course.'

'Garry, there's no need for that. Believe me, I'm
well and truly over that episode in my life.'

Frowning, he said, 'But my letter must have been an
awful shock to you. I—it was heartless and I'm sorry.
I could have told you more gently, more gradually.'

'It was a shock. And yes, you could have been
gentler about it, but what the hell does it matter now?'

He looked upset. 'You're bitter. I can't blame you.'

Ruth laughed as one might laugh at a joke one is

hearing for the third time. 'I'm not bitter. You see, I was never in love with you to begin with. I never loved you, though I confess it took me some time to realise it.'

She couldn't read his expression. Disbelief, relief, disappointment? 'I mean it, Garry. I have no hard feelings at all, I wouldn't be here if I had. I wish you and Angela all the very best. I hope you're happy together. I assume you plan to marry?'

They were interrupted by the arrival of a tea tray carried by a slightly unkempt waitress.

Garry reached for the teapot, as if wanting to busy himself. 'How many sugars?'

'I don't take sugar.'

'Oh, yes, I . . . My affair with Angela finished two months ago.'

Feeling a twinge of alarm, Ruth nodded. 'I see.' Surely, surely he didn't think he could resume his old relationship with her? 'And?'

'And I'm still in love with her.' For the first time, he allowed his feelings to show. He looked agonised.

'Oh, Garry! I'm so sorry.' She meant it; she knew only too well how he felt. 'Is that why you plan to live in London? To get away? Don't tell me Angela's from Wolverhampton?'

'No, no. Her home is in Scotland. She's still in Saudi, she's staying another year. She was dating a Norwegian doctor when I left. I begged her not to finish with me. I—I think I became an embarrassment to her.'

Ruth's eyes closed. Thank God she hadn't lost her dignity with Blake! It must be totally demoralising to know you've become an embarrassment to the person you're in love with, she thought, knowing a rush of sympathy for Garry. And what could she say to him? How could she assure him he'd get over it, that in time he'd forget Angela? She could hardly speak from experience. Would *she* ever get over Blake? 'I—know how you feel. I don't know what to say to you, Garry.'

'Which is why I had to talk to you.' He smiled then, as though he knew something she didn't. 'Having this happen to me made me realise how very deeply I'd hurt you, what I put you through. It feels like the end of the world, doesn't it? God, Ruth, I'm so sorry!'

It was seconds before she realised what was happening, how drastically they were failing to communicate. When she did see what was in Garry's mind, she wanted to laugh. But she didn't laugh. First, there was the danger she would be unable to stop, that she would laugh hysterically if she let her control slip, second, she didn't want to hurt Garry's feelings. He'd had enough of that from Angela.

A dozen thoughts flicked through her mind. She had been going to tell him about Blake, that she had learned the real meaning of love, what it felt like when one was really in love, that she had never known such emotions with him. But it was clear now that he hadn't believed her a moment ago, when she'd assured him she'd never really loved him. He simply had not believed her! He'd thought her motivated by pride.

She looked at him, feeling, now, very sorry for him. 'You're right,' she said, 'it does feel like the end of the world.'

'I'm sorry,' he said again, and she let him. How delicate the male ego, she thought. Let him think what he will. There's nothing to be gained by telling him about Blake. Just as Garry believed she had really loved him, he'd assume she'd fallen for her boss on the rebound.

She reached for her bag. She and Garry had nothing more to say to one another. There was no point in lingering.

'Ruth! You're not going? I thought—I thought we might go out for a meal later. I'd like to know how you're getting on, about your new life. I thought——'

Seeing her shaking her head slowly, he stopped. 'I'm being selfish. You're right, Ruth. I—I've no wish to open old wounds.' He looked at her sympathetically—and she let him. Since Angela didn't love him, what harm was there in letting him believe that she, Ruth, still did?

'I . . . was going to ask if we could meet from time to time,' he went on, avoiding her eyes now. 'When I move to London. Just as friends. But that wouldn't work, would it? It wouldn't be fair to you.'

'No,' she said softly, 'it wouldn't.'

He shoved his hands into the pockets of his slacks. It was a familiar gesture to her, something he did when he was tense. 'I hope you didn't mind my ringing you at work. I carefully didn't give my name.'

'No. Nobody knew who I was talking to.'

'And you're not angry with Pamela?'

Pamela Jeffries worked at the Building Society where Ruth had worked. 'Not at all. I never told anyone to keep my whereabouts from you. But how did Pamela know I was working for Marsden Toys?'

'Your mum had mentioned it, one day when she was in the Building Society.'

'Oh. Ah, well,' she sighed. 'I must go.'

'Ruth——'

She turned, seeing sadness in his eyes. Poor Garry. 'I did love you, I want you to know that. I was going to marry you. I—hope it helps for you to know that.'

Marriage and love didn't always go hand in hand, though. It had just seemed like a good idea at the time, to both of them. Whether Garry meant what he'd just said or whether he was just being kind, she didn't know. But if he believed it, he was mistaken. He hadn't loved her any more than she'd loved him. She smiled to herself. He couldn't even remember she didn't smoke, that she took her tea without sugar. 'Thank you. It does help.'

They'd had the room to themselves until then. Someone came in, an elderly lady carrying a Yorkshire terrier.

'Well, goodbye, Garry.'

'I'll walk to the door with you.'

As she was halfway down the hotel steps, she turned to him suddenly. 'Garry, I suppose you and Angela were lovers?'

He answered without thought. 'Of course.'

She was smiling to herself again. There was no 'of course' about it. She and he hadn't been lovers. There had been no particular passion in their relationship. 'But that wasn't enough, was it?'

'It never can be. The physical attraction between us was unlike anything I'd ever experienced. But I wanted more of her than that. I wanted to marry her. She, on the other hand, wasn't in love with me. So,' he shrugged, 'it could never have worked. For either of us.'

'You'll meet someone else. Someone who's right for you in every way.'

'The same goes for you, Ruth.'

With a little wave, she walked away. She walked aimlessly for a long time, content to do so. She was in no hurry to get home. In rhythm with every step she took, every click of her heels against the pavement, Blake's name echoed in her head.

She didn't regret her meeting with Garry; it had been worth coming into London for. In a way, it had been good for both of them, nice that they could meet to say goodbye on a friendly note.

How different it had been with Blake! Their

goodbye had been awful, the inevitable result of the
steady deterioration in their friendship.

Friendship. Yes, they had been friends. Quite apart
from the physical attraction, there had been friendship,
laughter, fun, trust. Blake had confided in her about
his past, his family ... but he had never told her
personally about his plan to retire next year. That
information had come from Dinah.

Why hadn't he told her? She shivered, though the
day was not cold. Because it hadn't suited him to, that
was why! Telling her would have made it clear she
couldn't expect an ongoing relationship with him, so it
hadn't suited him to tell her. He knew her well, he'd
known she wasn't the type of girl who would embark
on an affair when the end of it was already in sight!

In this, they were different, very different. Blake's
attitude towards sex was casual. She had to say one
thing for him: at least he was open about it, honest
about it. 'You're still in love with Garry,' he'd said,
'yet you want me, physically. And why fight it?'

Without realising it, Ruth quickened her steps. She
felt angry. How blasé Blake had been! How simply
black-and-white it had all seemed to him. But it wasn't
that simple for her.

When she thought of his offhand, ridiculous
proposal of marriage, she got angrier, then she laughed
aloud. What would he have done if she'd called his
bluff? 'I want you,' he'd said, 'doesn't that say it all?'

Yes, come to think about it, it certainly did say it all!
She hadn't realised before how significant that silly
proposal was, it told her things about Blake which
she'd never realised, never thought about before. The
man had never been in love in his entire life, he
couldn't have been! For all his experience, for all his
women, he had reached the age of thirty-four without
once falling in love. If he had, he wouldn't have

proposed to someone he didn't love. With the exception of marriages of convenience or the seeking solely of companionship or money, how could anyone who had known love marry without it?

Ruth stopped in her tracks, her eyes riveted to the pavement. There was a possible alternative: maybe Blake loved her. She dismissed that particular thought instantly as wishful thinking. She walked on, laughing aloud again, a hollow, sad sound. How wishful can you get? she asked herself. Just how carried away can you get?

For all her sensitivity and sentimentality, there was also a realistic, practical side to her nature. She, personally, would never, ever marry unless she at least believed herself to be in love. It wouldn't work otherwise.

Gasping, staggering backwards, she realised she had walked straight into someone. A policeman, of all people! She muttered her apologies rapidly, looking around, realising where she was. She didn't need to be a Londoner to recognise Buckingham Palace. It was just across the road, looking magnificent in bright, October sunlight.

'Are you all right, miss?' The policeman put a steadying hand on her arm.

'Y-yes, I'm so sorry, I was—looking for the Underground.'

His eyes moved swiftly over her, with admiration rather than suspicion, before he directed her to the station.

She hurried away, feeling idiotic, getting more and more angry with Blake Marsden by the minute. Well, that was *it*. She wasn't going to think about him any more. She had faced facts: even if Blake had been prepared to marry her, he'd been talking of nothing more than legalised sex.

With a shudder of distaste, she quickened her steps again.

CHAPTER TWELVE

'TABATHA, I'm going to work on Monday. Will you miss me, not having me at home all day?' Distractedly, Ruth lifted her cat off her lap. She was sitting in an armchair, her eyes fixed on the painting above the fireplace, the painting Blake had given to her, his painting. It was beautiful, done in oils, an autumn scene in the woods. She had put it on her wall, given it pride of place, the night he'd given it to her.

'Dammit, Tabby, I've got to stop this, I know I have.' She was crying again. She had spent part of every day crying, every day of the last two weeks. Keeping Blake from her thoughts had been easier said than done. It was impossible. He was in her mind every waking moment and often in her dreams. And they were troubled dreams, always, when Blake was in them. Often they were so jumbled, so disturbing they would wake her up, and then she would cry again.

For two solid weeks she had been nowhere except the supermarket, seen no one. Both Wendy and Derek had phoned and begged her to visit in the first few days after she'd left Marsdens, but she had declined. She had asked them to leave her alone for a while, assuring them she was all right, that she simply needed to be alone. They had understood, as she had known they would, but had not approved.

Her parents knew what was happening. Wendy had told them. Ruth didn't mind, she'd have told them herself if necessary; her sister-in-law had made it easier for her, sparing her the necessity of talking about Blake.

She didn't want to talk about him. Not to anyone.

But her brother had phoned her last night and insisted she visit this week-end. She was going to. She would go for dinner tomorrow, Sunday.

It was a small concession to please her loved ones, it had been a small decision to make, that she would go to see them. And yet, having made the decision, she had felt surprisingly better for a while, just for an hour or two. For a little while she had thought not of Blake but of herself and what she was doing.

What she was doing was pointless, self-destructive. So, she had decided, she would go to the agency on Monday, to ask for work. And she would go to her class at night-school next week. She had enrolled for dressmaking classes but she'd skipped the past three weeks.

The telephone rang. She reached for it, knowing it would be one of her parents. Today was Saturday.

Christmas was mentioned. It was November now, and her mother wanted to know whether she had any plans. Plans? No, none at all. Nor did she have any enthusiasm, for Christmas or anything else. But she tried not to show this in her voice. Her parents were marvellous, avoiding any mention of Blake or anything connected with him. She had to make an effort for their sake, she didn't want them to worry about her any more than they were already worrying.

'I haven't given it a thought, Mum. I don't mind, I'll be happy to come home. There's only the one bedroom here so—unless you're planning to go to Derek's? Have you spoken to them about it?'

'No, I'm going to ring them in a minute. I'll see what Wendy thinks.' A tinge of worry showed in Norma Boyd's voice. 'Is she looking well, Ruth? Derek says so but what do you think?'

'I—haven't seen them for a couple of weeks. I'm

going to have a meal with them tomorrow. Now Mum, don't start worrying about Wendy and the baby. I promise you, the last time I saw her she was glowing, just like pregnant women are supposed to.'

Her mother laughed at that. 'I never glowed! I had a heck of a time with you and Derek and Helen!'

'Ah, but we were worth it, weren't we?'

'That you were. Are. All right, love, I'll ring off now and talk to your brother. Oh, Ruth, are you still there? Listen, your Dad and I are sending you a little something. We know how much you'd like to get your own car and——'

'Oh, *no*, Mum! You and Dad have done enough for me, you must keep your money for Christmas. Honestly, it's not as if I *need* a car.'

No, but it would be nice, very handy. She put the phone down, wishing her mother were here in the room with her. She was feeling so very vulnerable just now, so emotionally delicate that the idea of giving and getting a hug from her mum brought fresh tears to her eyes. God, she was fed up! She really would make an effort now. She really would go to the agency on Monday.

In fact she got moving there and then. She did some hand-washing, put a load in the washing-machine and vacuumed throughout the flat, all jobs which were way overdue. She felt a bit better, more cheerful. Her parents would send the cheque regardless, she knew. Her protests wouldn't stop them. And, maybe, together with her own small savings their help would enable her to put a deposit on something decent. She had wanted a car of her own since the day she'd passed her driving test . . . Blake, Blake, what a lovely evening we had, celebrating. I wonder if you remember it? Oh, *Blake*!

Almost desperately, she shoved the vacuum around

the floor like one who was in a dire hurry. She had to get busy and keep busy. She mustn't think of him, it hurt too much, it was a real, physical pain. She must rise above it, enjoy the idea that she might be able to buy a car.

All her savings had gone on the flat, she had put down as much money as possible in order to keep her mortgage low. All she had kept back was money for furniture and a washing-machine and things. Since then, while working at—while working as a secretary—she'd started to build her savings up again. Then she'd dipped in to them to buy a TV and some nice clothes for ... some nice clothes to wear at work.

'Nice dress, Ruth. You look lovely.' Derek looked at her approvingly when she took off her coat the next day. 'Give me that, I'll hang it up for you. Wendy's in the kitchen. We'll go in there, shall we? See if she wants a hand.'

Derek was a good husband. He'd been making certain his wife didn't overdo things during this pregnancy.

'Hi!' Wendy looked up, smiling. 'Ruth, you look smashing. Gorgeous dress! It looks expensive.'

It had been. It was cashmere, burgundy-coloured, and Blake had admired it ... 'Here, let me do that.'

'I don't want any fussing. I've been sitting down all day, honestly.'

Ruth looked to her brother. He nodded. 'I have permitted her to make dinner,' he said grandly, much to the women's amusement.

It was a fairly successful evening. Taboo subjects were not mentioned. Christmas was discussed. It had been decided between Wendy and her mother-in-law that everyone would go to Wolverhampton for the occasion.

'Seems fair,' Ruth remarked. 'You had us all here last year.'

Wendy smiled knowingly. She really was looking well, getting very large around the middle. 'Mum didn't really ask me so much as tell me. You watch, I'll bet she won't let me lift a teaspoon while we're there.'

'Will you mind?'

'No, bless her. All I want is to deliver a healthy, beautiful new grandchild for her.' A shadow crossed her face, a fleeting doubt which was plain to see. After three miscarriages, it was understandable.

'You will, darling.' Derek reassured her. 'You will.'

'What about your parents, Wendy?' Ruth brought the subject back to Christmas, not wanting Wendy to dwell on negative thoughts. 'What are they doing for Christmas?'

'They're going to my sister, in Cornwall. Which reminds me, have you sent anything to Helen? When's the last date for sending parcels to Australia, do you know?'

Ruth put her hand to her mouth. 'No! I mean, no I haven't. I don't know. It must be any day now. Heavens, I'd better do something about that. I haven't given it a thought.'

There was another knowing look from Wendy, though she said nothing. Both she and Derek knew it was out of character for Ruth to forget her sister and her family in Australia. She had never neglected to send presents for birthdays and Christmas—and they had always been sent in good time.

How could one person have the power to do this to another person? How could the absence of one person make such a difference to one's life? To one's mind? To one's appetite ... sleep, incentive, energy, enthusiasm ...

Blake. Oh, *Blake*!

The answer was easy. As Garry had so succinctly described it, when you lose someone you love deeply, it feels like the end of the world.

But it isn't.

She looked at Derek, glanced at her watch. 'Can I beg a lift home? I know it's early but I want to wash my hair and sort myself out. I'm going back to work tomorrow.'

They looked pleased. Derek looked very pleased but Wendy—well, there was also just the slightest narrowing of her eyes, enough to tell Ruth she mustn't think she was fooling her.

Ruth did an about-face during the next three weeks. Whereas at first she had hidden herself away like a wounded animal, she spent the next three weeks being frantically busy, spending hardly any time in her flat. Apart from her one evening at night-school, she took herself off to the cinema or for a solitary meal or late-night shopping, or both. She went often to her relatives and had two evenings out with girls from the office where she was temping. But she refused the offer of a blind date. She refused three direct offers from men in the company, men whose interest left her cold.

She had tucked away the money her parents had sent to her, which was to be her Christmas present. She was still toying with the idea of getting a car but, really, she didn't exactly need one. Granted, commuting to work was sometimes a chilly business these November days but the transport services were reliable. Besides, what fun would there be in driving around alone? For her, that would not be a pleasure.

She was not happy with her own company. She needed people, at least occasionally. Nor had she ever been happy living alone. But it was necessary, so that was that. She was too old to go back to Mum and Dad. And there was, after all, Wendy and Derek when she needed company. This was one reason she hadn't thought of moving away from the area. She had done that once before, hadn't she? Run away from things familiar, from memories? She did, of course, dread the idea of running into Blake. That was the last thing she wanted. She felt sure that if he saw her now, if they came face to face, he would know how she felt. She would break down, she felt certain of it, she would wear her heart on her sleeve, her love for him in her eyes.

But she had seen no one from Marsden's, not Dinah or Rory or any of the others. They all lived within a radius of some twenty miles, but that was a lot of space. Besides, the factory was out of town, on a route she never travelled these days. The chances of bumping into one of the Marsdens in town was remote, too. Both Dagenham and Ilford were very big places.

But they weren't big enough.

On the first Saturday in December, in Ilford, that which Ruth had dreaded, happened.

Her quest for Christmas presents had taken her in and out of more than a dozen shops and stores, and by lunch-time she was famished. And her feet were aching.

Encumbered with several carrier bags which were bulky rather than heavy, Ruth stopped to look at the menu in the window of an inexpensive restaurant where she knew she would be served quickly. The place was packed, she saw that when her eyes moved from the menu to the window.

And then she saw Blake.

He was staring at her, his eyes narrowed as if he

were unsure it really was her. He was sitting at a table with two people unknown to Ruth, who might or might not have been strangers to him. People, perhaps, with whom he might have been sharing a table because the restaurant was so busy.

Those were her impressions as her eyes met with his. They looked at one another across a distance of some four or five tables in the crowded restaurant. As he got quickly to his feet, she saw his lips form the sound of her name—and she bolted.

She didn't run immediately, she walked briskly until she was out of his sight then she ran like the devil, down the street and through the swing doors of a department store. She lost herself immediately in the crowd, gasping for air, her heart banging frantically in her breast.

Like a criminal, she scanned the faces around her, feeling afraid. He had come out of the restaurant, she felt certain, she could tell from the way he'd stood, moved, that he'd intended to pursue her. He was probably looking for her in the shop next door now; she hadn't let him see her running.

Five minutes passed before she felt secure, before she steadied herself—before she realised she was standing in a toy department. The place was packed with children and adults alike, with train sets whirring, toy dogs yapping, rubber ducks quacking and dolls crying as the department's goodies were demonstrated and inspected by staff and customers. And there, sure enough, sitting appealingly on a shelf was a range of Marsden's teddies.

Not one of them had sly eyes.

CHAPTER THIRTEEN

CHRISTMAS was without joy. That was not the way Ruth behaved but it was the way she felt. It was the first time she had been back to Wolverhampton since moving south and it seemed strange to be sleeping in her own bed in her own room, a room she had once shared with her sister Helen. When Derek had left the family nest to go away to university, she and Helen had had a room each, they had flipped a coin to decide who would take over their brother's room. Helen had. For a time, as teenagers, they had missed one another at night, missed the secret exchange of secret news which invariably involved the opposite sex, the latest heart-throb.

Now, at bedtime on Christmas Eve, Ruth looked round her room and smiled at the memories it held for her. She still missed her sister, she always had. She would be ringing from Australia tomorrow, as she always did on Christmas Day, and everyone would have a word with her. They would queue up by the telephone, waiting their turn, and the exchanges would be brief because the call would be expensive.

'I'm a different person,' Ruth wanted to say when her turn came, when her sister would ask how she was. 'I've never been so unhappy in my life. I'm in love with a man who couldn't care less whether I live or die, someone who once made me happy, who changed me into a more positive person only to eject me later from his life and leave me without a shred of confidence.'

Of course she said no such thing when her turn

came the next day. She spoke to her sister with the cheerfulness she was showing to the rest of her family.

She had been making a consistent effort to behave cheerfully over Christmas and she was doing well. She fooled everyone except Wendy.

Though nothing was said, the others seemed to believe she was getting over her one-sided love affair. But her sighting of Blake at the start of the month had upset her all over again. She had been getting herself together, knocking her life into shape, and it had put her back to square one. Seeing him had resurrected the hurt she had begun to sublimate. She had been in pain for the rest of that day, that evening.

Like a fool she'd sat by her telephone that night, waiting for it to ring. Willing it to ring. She had run from Blake without thinking about what she was doing. She had panicked at the sight of him. It had shaken her even more than she would have believed possible.

Then, later, she had regretted her action. What if he'd wanted to say something more than a mere hello to her? What if there were some hope that . . . well, he knew her address, she'd reasoned. He had her telephone number.

So she had sat by the phone, not just for that evening but for the entire weekend. Literally, like one obsessed, she had stayed by the phone all day Sunday except for excursions to the bathroom. She hadn't cooked herself a meal, she hadn't even got dressed.

But neither Blake nor anyone else had phoned that day.

At five minutes to midnight she'd gone to bed, having waited for 'just another half-hour' several times. She had been guilty of wishful thinking again. She had been mistaken. If Blake had wanted to say anything at all to her, he could have phoned. No doubt he had sat down to finish his meal when he'd seen her walk away.

She had had a Christmas card from Marsden's, an impersonal thing with the company address printed on it. It had been signed, Blake, Rory and Dinah—in Dinah's hand. Blake probably didn't even know it had been sent.

Millie had sent a card, too. 'Things aren't the same around here since you left,' she'd written on it. 'Life is by no means as pleasant. Give me a ring sometime, perhaps we can get together for a drink?' And she had put her home telephone number underneath this.

Ruth had sent a card in return but she hadn't phoned. It was sweet of Millie to write a note implying she missed her but the suggestion of getting together for a drink was probably just politeness on Millie's part. She wasn't free during the evenings or even at lunch-times. Besides, apart from working at Marsden's, she and Millie had nothing in common, they had been friends only in the sphere of work.

On New Year's Eve, Norma and Reginald Boyd had a small party. Mrs Edwards, the old lady from next door, came with her niece, who was staying with her for a few days. Two married couples came, other neighbours Ruth had known a long time, and they, together with the Boyd family, made a merry group who celebrated into the early hours.

The strain of appearing happy was catching up with Ruth by then and she wished herself elsewhere. Putting on a false front was exhausting. She wanted to go to bed by ten o'clock but of course that was out of the question. She had been elected as the one who would bring in the New Year when the clock struck twelve.

At two minutes to midnight she stood outside on the street, shivering against the cold night air and wondering what the New Year held in store for her. Well, she supposed, that would depend on her. One thing was for sure, she had to snap herself out of this awful lethargy. She had to learn to be interested in things again. She had to learn to live again, to come *alive* again. She wasn't even sure who she was any more, her confidence had disintegrated. Being rejected by two men was not good for any girl's self-image. She hadn't even been able to hold Garry's interest once he'd gone to Saudi. It had been a case of out of sight, out of mind, even with him. So how could she possibly have hoped a man like Blake Marsden would learn to love her?

Wendy went to bed just after midnight. She was just over six months pregnant. She was keeping very well and looking it, she was still driving her car to and from the shops at home, but she was easily tired. She took a nap during the day, and staying up to let the New Year in was as much as she could manage. Ruth made her excuses half an hour later, by then she was feeling almost desperate to escape to the privacy of her room. She was on the verge of tears again and, tonight, she didn't think she could hold them back.

She lay down on her bed and gave vent to them, crying into her pillow in an effort to muffle any sound. Would it never stop, this awful, gnawing ache inside her? It had been a little less than three months since she'd left Marsden's but it felt like three years, three years during which she had aged twenty.

By one-thirty the house was quiet. So, too, was Ruth. Tired though she was, she couldn't sleep tonight. She tried to read but it didn't help. How could it when she couldn't concentrate on the words before her? At a little after two she got out of bed and went down to make herself some tea. She moved quietly, not wishing to disturb anyone.

Tabatha greeted her as she went into the kitchen. There had been nobody with whom Ruth could leave her at Pine Court, or rather nobody she would trust, so Tabby had been brought here for the celebrations.

'Some celebrations, eh, Tabs?' Ruth poured a saucer of milk for her before putting the kettle on. 'It's been hard work hasn't it, trying to pretend everything's all right?'

'Very hard, I should think.'

She turned, startled to hear Wendy's voice behind her. 'Oh, no! I woke you. I'm sorry, Wendy, I——'

'No, no, you didn't wake me. This often happens. I have a couple of hours sleep and then I wake up full of beans.' She grinned. 'Though on this occasion, somebody else woke me—and I don't mean you. Here.' She took Ruth's hand and put it on her huge stomach. 'Could you sleep with that going on inside you? When he kicks, he kicks! I think I've got a budding half-back in there!'

'Or a champion hockey player, perhaps?' Fascinated, Ruth smiled in awe. 'Oh, Wendy, isn't that amazing? Does it hurt?'

'Not exactly. Well, sort of. Yes and no.'

'How very informative!'

Wendy giggled. 'Well, perhaps that's because it's a discomfort I'm very happy to put up with.' She sat down at the kitchen table. 'I'll have a cuppa if you're making one.'

'You sure you're feeling all right?'

'Very sure. I only wish I could say the same for you. Isn't it time you talked to me, Ruth? Can you, now? You've never told me the full story of what happened the day you left Marsden's. I've been afraid to ask until now, I didn't want to upset you by——'

'I know. I'm sorry about that. Yes, I think I can tell

you everything now. I—I want to. I think talking about it will help.'

'That's what I'm here for.'

Ruth smiled gratefully. Wendy was like a sister to her. For all Ruth knew, Wendy had come downstairs deliberately for this, to give her the opportunity to talk in private. And she hadn't talked before, she had been unable to, unable to tell anything but the skimpiest details. Wendy didn't even know what had been said at her meeting with Garry.

An hour and two cups of tea later, she knew everything. Ruth described how life had been in the office, how strained and awful the atmosphere had been between her and Blake. 'Ever since we came back from Rome. Nothing had been the same since then. I'm sure he'd thought I was going to start an affair with him while we were away. Maybe that's why he took me with him.' She retracted those words instantly. 'No, forget that, Wendy. That's not fair. I worked damned hard there and without wishing to sound immodest, I don't know how he'd have managed without me. It was . . .' Her voice trailed off. She struggled to compose herself even though she felt sure there couldn't actually be any more tears in her. Surely, surely there were no tears left? It was just that all this was so difficult to cope with, to understand . . . 'We had such fun that day we went sightseeing in Rome. I felt so close to Blake then, I—I really don't know what went wrong.'

'Yes, you do.' Wendy looked at her sadly. 'You've already answered that question, Ruth.'

'So I have.' She got up. There were a few bottles on the draining-board, leftovers from the party. 'I think I'll have something a bit stronger to drink. Maybe it'll help me sleep.'

'Blake didn't know you were going to meet Garry, did he?'

'No, no way. Nobody knew. Not that I've anything to hide, it just didn't seem . . . tactful. 'Course I realise now he wouldn't have given a damn.'

Wendy looked a little bemused. 'I don't know why you bothered going to see Garry. You don't owe him anything, far from it.'

'I know that. It—well, there was no harm in it. We left on a good note, having cleared the air, sort of thing. Besides, he happened to be in London and if nothing else, it gave me something to do that day, got me out of my flat. I felt sorry for Garry, I knew only too well how he was feeling. I *know* only too well.'

Reaching over to squeeze her hand, Wendy sighed and shook her head. 'I've been so lucky myself. I never went through anything like this, but I can sympathise. I can imagine how you feel. Derek and I—it was right between us from the beginning. And we both knew it, thank goodness. Tra, la, we fell in love and we're still in love.'

Without envy, Ruth said, 'Yes. You have been lucky in that respect.' She sat back in her chair. 'It does hurt, Wendy, it hurts like hell. But I will get over it. I know I will. I *have* to. I—I just *wish* I hadn't gone into Ilford shopping that day. Coming across Blake like that——'

'Don't be silly! You can't live your life trying to avoid someone. You can't hibernate because there's just a chance you'll bump into Blake.' With a sudden, forceful exclamation, she added, 'Honestly, I could kill him! He doesn't know what he's missing! I know he's very shrewd in business but I must say he didn't strike me as the calculating type. But he is, obviously. I think his asking you to marry him like that was very unkind. It was that that made things a hundred times worse between you. Things might have picked up again, nature, or something, might have taken its course if he hadn't shown himself to be an absolute stinker. He was just dangling a carrot at you and believe me, if you had called his bluff, nothing would have come of it.'

'You think I don't know that?' Ruth laughed. 'Take my word for it, Wendy, I've been over the entire thing a million times in my head. I've dissected, I've analysed. He just wanted an affair and, since I wouldn't play ball, he then decided to get me out of his life. Maybe it was more than his ego could stand, having me around in the office—the one who got away, if you see what I mean.'

'I told you——'

'I know, I know. I know what you're going to say.' Ruth remembered only too clearly a conversation she'd had weeks earlier with her sister-in-law. 'You said I'd end up leaving Marsden's—for one reason or another.'

After a moment's silence, Ruth went on. 'At least I kept my pride, my dignity. At least he never knew how I felt about him. That's why I had to get out of his sight when I saw him in Ilford. I knew that if I came face to face with him, he'd be able to see how I felt. I'd been so upset, was so upset, it would have shown on my face.'

'You did the right thing,' Wendy agreed. 'Getting away. It was best not to speak to him. You're right, it does show in your face, your eyes. Your feelings show when you speak of him, it's happening now and it always has. I knew long before you did that you were in love with him.'

When Ruth caught the other woman stifling a yawn, she felt guilty. 'Look at you! Oh, Wendy, I'm being very selfish, you must go back to bed. You need your rest.'

'Are you coming?'

'Soon. I'll just finish this drink.'

'Ruth, love, I don't think——'

'No, it's all right.' She could guess what Wendy was thinking. 'I'm not going to drink myself into a stupor, don't worry about that. Unfortunately, I can't handle much drink—otherwise I might!'

Wendy still hesitated, hovering by the door. 'Come to bed then. You can take that with you.'

Ruth gave in. She didn't want Wendy worrying about her. As they reached the landing, she kissed her good night, whispering, 'Thanks, Wendy. It did help, talking to you about it.'

And so it had, a little. But it didn't solve anything.

The inevitable television advertisements for holidays had been driving all of them mad over Christmas and the New Year. Still, they had the desired effect because the subject of holidays was discussed, but Ruth was really the only one in the market. With the arrival of the baby in March, a summer holiday was out of the question as far as Wendy and Derek were concerned.

For Norma and Reginald it was out of the question financially. They were both retired and, having spent so much money on their trip to Australia, they had to 'pull in their horns a bit,' as Reg put it.

'You're due for a holiday, though,' he told Ruth. 'You haven't had one in—what? Two years or more.'

Business trips to Rome didn't count.

'I'll think about it, Dad. It might be nice to get a car instead, before the summer starts. We'll see. It'll be a car or a holiday, anyway.'

'Have you anywhere in mind?' Derek asked. 'I want to know which advert's worked on you!'

Anywhere except Greece. 'If I go, I'll go where there's guaranteed sunshine.' But not to Greece. Was Blake there now, in Greece for the holidays? Staying in his new house? Practising for his retirement?

It was very difficult to imagine him retired. She stopped trying.

Mrs Edwards put an end to that particular conversation. She descended on the Boyds again on New Year's day, as she'd been invited to, with her niece.

On the morning of the following day, Ruth, Derek and Wendy headed for home in Derek's car. It had been a nice, normal, family Christmas as far as everyone else was concerned. Though she had been troubled, Ruth herself felt sorry to be leaving now the time had come.

Tabatha was on the back seat with her as they drove south, in her special cat-box, and her owner just managed to stop herself in time before saying something tactless in front of Wendy and Derek. She'd always talked aloud to her cat, ever since she got her, and she'd been about to remark to Tabby that there wasn't much waiting for them at home.

Still, who knew what the new year would bring? After all, when she thought back over what had happened to her during the course of last year, nothing should surprise her. If things had gone according to plan and Fate had not taken a hand, she'd be married to Garry Anderson now and living in that little house on the new estate.

She shuddered at the thought.

The new year would certainly bring a new job, if nothing else. A permanent one. She would take her time, carry on temping while looking for the perfect permanent job. Maybe she would find something where there'd be some travelling involved. That would be nice.

The flat felt empty, unlived-in, cold. Ruth turned the central-heating on full, fed her cat then popped out for a newspaper. She might as well start scanning the situations vacant column straight away. Shivering in the freezing January air, she decided it would be a car this year, not a holiday. Gosh, it was cold, so cold her limbs felt stiff.

She ran home, locked her doors, made herself some coffee and pored over the paper.

That turned out to be what she did almost every evening during the bitterly cold January days which followed. She would get home from work, make coffee and scan the paper, pausing every now and then to ask Tabatha's opinion on a job advertisement. 'How does this sound, Tabby? Secretary required . . .'

One evening at the end of January, she answered herself on her pet's behalf. 'It sounds positively boring. Just like you do! Why don't you do something different? You don't have to work as a secretary, do you? You could work in—in a shop or a boutique or something, mix with the public. Have a change. You're in a rut. Come to think of it, you are pathetic. You keep spotting potentially suitable jobs but you never apply for them. You keep moving from office to office, it's no wonder you have no girlfriends. There's no time for friendships to develop. Worse, you're behaving like an old maid. A dotty old maid, at that. Look at you! If anyone could see you now, they'd think you're nuts. You're twenty-three years old—well, you will be at the beginning of March, and you sit home night after night talking to a dumb animal.'

She looked at Tabatha solemnly. 'You're absolutely right.'

Her birthday, the 3rd of March, was the date Wendy had been given for the arrival of her baby, which was a thought that pleased Ruth. She glanced at her watch. Wendy would be here in an hour or so, she should get a move on. For once she wasn't going to spend her evening reading and watching TV. At least, not all of it.

The doorbell rang. 'That's Wendy, Tabs. Derek's gone to a meeting straight from work tonight, so Wendy's dining with us.' She glanced at her watch again as she got up. 'She's early, it's only six o'clock! She said she'd be here at seven. Honestly, I don't know how she manages to drive in her condition, I mean, she's so *big* now. Surely she'll have to give it up any minute now.'

It seemed curious for Wendy to be an hour out in her timing. Ruth had been in for half an hour but she hadn't started preparations for dinner yet. She should have got cracking in the kitchen as soon as she got home, but she had settled down with coffee and the paper and . . . time had slipped by.

Time stood still when she opened the door.

Everything stopped, the world, her breathing, her heartbeat.

Blake Marsden was on her doorstep, not Wendy, and he was smiling at her. A tender smile. 'Hello, Ruth,' he said.

CHAPTER FOURTEEN

RUTH's lips parted but not a sound came past them. Her hand tightened on the doorknob. Towering over her, his fathomless blue eyes looking straight at her, Blake seemed as large as life. Yet she couldn't believe he was here.

'I want to talk to you, Ruth. May I come in?'

She gasped softly, feeling light-headed, short of oxygen. He was here. It was him. It was not a mirage. He was here, clad in a heavy, navy-blue overcoat, frowning worriedly at her now, but no, he couldn't come in. What kind of sadist was he? What kind of sick joke was this? There was a banging sound in her ears as her circulation steadied itself, but she was far from steady. She felt as though a scream were trying to form itself inside her. 'What—what do you want, Blake?'

'You,' he said simply. He reached out a hand, was about to touch her face.

Ruth jerked backwards as if he'd struck her. 'Go away. I have nothing to say to you, nothing!'

It was as though he hadn't heard her protest. 'You,' he said again, his voice strangely soft. ' I want to talk to you, I want to take you in my arms, I want to hear you say you'll marry me and spend every day of the rest of your life with me.'

With an unnatural calmness she turned away from him and walked back to her living-room. She heard his close the door as he followed her, she heard him hang up his overcoat in the small hallway. This, while at the same time she was aware of the way her hands had started to tremble, of the blood draining from her face. She could feel it happening to her. She had heard his words, she had allowed him into her home not because they meant anything but because she felt sure she would scream . . . if the sound could get past the constriction in her throat. When it happened, she didn't want to be standing in such very clear earshot of her neighbours.

Physically unable to stay on her feet, she sat in an armchair. Tabatha jumped immediately on to her lap. Automatically, Ruth reached out a hand to stroke her, allowing her eyes to close. Perhaps when she opened them again, Blake would be gone.

He wasn't.

He was sitting, watching her. 'I'm sorry. Maybe I should have phoned to announce my arrival. Ruth—' He dropped his head into his hands, his fingers digging into the thick, black hair. 'I don't know how to begin. We've both lost about four months of our lives because somehow we've failed to communicate, because you never gave me the slightest sign that you love me.'

Ruth's hands tightened around her cat. Very calmly, almost inaudibly she said, 'I don't love you, Blake. I can't imagine how you've got that idea.'

'No? You always were a lousy liar, my darling girl.' He shook his head solemnly. He looked leaner than he had when last she saw him—before the incident in the restaurant, that was. To one who didn't know every angle of his face, every last nuance of his features, he might have appeared unchanged.

But Ruth was aware of his weight-loss, aware that he was tired. The bones of his face were just a touch more prominent and around his eyes there were faint lines of strain.

Determined not to avert her eyes, she continued

looking at him. To avoid his scrutiny would be to add fuel to his last statement. He had made that statement sadly, not angrily, yet the set of his mouth spoke of his annoyance. Whether it was directed at her or at himself, she didn't know. On one tier of her mind she was laughing at herself because there had been a time, a long time ago, when she had thought he had a mean mouth. How odd that she had once thought that. Of course, she hadn't known him then, she hadn't known how determined a character he was, and how proud. Nor had she known how much passion that mouth could create and enjoy.

'It's no use looking at me like that, Ruth. Your feelings for me are written all over your face. You're in love with me. God in heaven, *why* didn't you tell me? Why did you let me believe you were still in love with Anderson? Couldn't you at least have told me that much, that you felt nothing for him any more?'

So his anger was directed at her. 'Please go, Blake. You're upsetting me more than you can imagine, and it's pointless.'

'Pointless? More than I can imagine? What the hell do you think I've been going through these past months? I've been dying inside, dying! I've cursed the day I ever set eyes on you and I've made the lives of everyone around me a misery! More than I can imagine? What do you think I'm made of—steel?'

Ruth's eyes had widened in alarm, she was alarmed because a feeling of hope had forced its way inside her. Surely he couldn't mean it? He was talking like—like a man in love. Oh, she had seen him angry before, plenty of times; she had seen him talk with passion before, when discussing business or painting or politics ... but ... but never about his feelings. Not feelings like this. He had never let her know she had the power to affect him in any way except the physical.

'Well, I'm not, I assure you,' he went on more quietly. 'I'm not as vulnerable as some, but I am human. And I'm very vulnerable where you're concerned. I always have been, right from the start.'

Tabatha was squirming on her knee. She released her and watched in mild astonishment as her pet went straight to Blake, nuzzling against his legs as if to show that her sympathies were with him.

And then he smiled. 'You see? Even your Tabby is on my side!'

Something crumbled inside her. She leaned forward, as though in pain, her arms wrapped tightly around her midriff. 'I—I really can't talk to you now, Blake.' Talk to him? She couldn't even think straight. 'I'm—somebody's coming. Wendy. I—she's coming for dinner.'

'Wendy isn't coming for dinner.'

'Yes, she'll be here any minute and believe me, you won't be a welcome sight to her.'

'Ruth, look at me. Look at me,' he coaxed. 'Wendy is the reason I'm here.'

'What—what do you mean?'

'I mean it's thanks to her concern for you that I'm sitting here now.'

Oh, God, no! She couldn't bear it. If Wendy had got in touch with Blake, she would die. Surely, surely she wouldn't do that? Surely her worry wasn't such that she would ring Blake and tell him how Ruth had been drowning . . .

'And make no mistake,' he went on, a wry smile pulling at his mouth. 'I wasn't a welcome sight to her. I happened to see her in town a couple of hours ago. She'd been shopping. I said hello, offered to carry her bag to the car park for her—huge lady that she is—and she hissed at me that she could manage perfectly well, thank you very much. I knew instantly I was a villain but I didn't know why.

'Suffice it to say we had a cup of coffee together and the whole story came out. When she started to tell me . . . Ruth? Oh, Ruth, darling, don't!'

Without the remotest semblance of dignity, she had started to cry, loud, helpless, snuffly sobs she couldn't get under control. '*Don't!*' As Blake made a move towards her, she thrust her arm up. 'Don't touch me. Don't, please. Please.'

'Ruth——'

'Please!' Had she been looking at him she'd have seen that he, too, looked helpless now. 'I can't bear it, Blake. I'm too tender, too sore, I don't want you to touch me.'

'What—I don't understand. What does that mean?'

She flung her head back, tears streaking down her face. 'It means I love you, you idiot. It means I'm so in love with you I can't even—not when . . .' Her voice broke.

Blake was beside her in a flash, kneeling, holding her so tightly she felt her ribs would break. Yet she couldn't get enough of it. She wanted him to hold her like this, tight, tighter, until the sun lost its warmth, until hell froze over.

With her cheek beside his he held her until, finally, she stopped crying. He fished in his pocket, one arm still around her. 'Here, blow, my foolish darling.'

She blew, noisily, hiccupping once or twice.

His long fingers cupped her chin, lifting her face to his. 'Look at those eyes. Oh, how they've haunted me!' With a gentle smile, he admonished her. 'How dare you call me an idiot? You're the idiot. You deceived me and I've always prided myself on being aware of female deceptions, aware and impervious. Ah, did I have a lot to learn!' Very seriously, he added, 'It's going to take me a long time to explain to you how much you've taught me, my darling.'

'I—hiccup—have?'

'Indeed. Hiccup!'

She put both her hands on his face, laughing now. 'Get me a drink, would you?'

'Not till you've kissed me.'

It was several minutes before she got her drink. She kissed him tenderly, she kissed him expressively, so that he would really understand how she felt about him, so that he would know all the things she had never been able to tell him before.

When the kiss changed to one of hunger, subtly but inevitably, Blake pulled away. He stood, one dark eyebrow raised, one long finger wagging at her. He didn't need actually to say anything.

She stifled a smile until he turned away. There was a modestly stocked drinks table by the fireplace and as Blake filled two glasses, Tabatha returned to her mistress.

'So we're friends again, are we?'

'What?' Blake turned, the contents of the glasses slopping perilously close to the rim. 'Oh! 'Tis she! Now listen, when we're married, I'm going to get a mate for that little animal of yours. She takes too much of your attention.'

'Why, Blake Marsden! I believe you're jealous.'

'Too right.'

'Of a cat?'

'Of anything you find as cuddlesome as I am.'

Ruth burst out laughing. 'Cuddlesome, you are not! There's no way I or anyone else could describe you as cuddlesome. Awesome, yes, but not——'

She was hauled to her feet. Unperturbed, Tabby was jettisoned and landed daintily on her feet.

Ruth landed up against the hardness of Blake's

chest. His fingers slid into her hair on both sides of her forehead, his eyes suddenly filled with pain. 'Why, Ruth? How the devil did this happen to us? All this time, and to think that if I hadn't bumped into Wendy ... *Why?*'

'Oh, Blake!' She sat on the sofa, near which he had placed the drinks. 'I don't know. There's so much— isn't Wendy coming round? Really?'

'Of course she isn't. She's getting her own dinner and she's more than happy to do so. Her last words to me were, "Tell Ruth I'll be in touch soon. Good luck, love. She's all yours now!" So you see, there are no problems with Wendy, for either of us.'

'Sounds like I've been given away!'

'No.' He sat, catching hold of her hand. 'You've been claimed. Now, why have I had to wait so long?'

'I could ask you the same question, Blake.'

'No, that's not fair. You let me believe you were in love with Garry. When he phoned you, when I heard you making a date with him, realised he was coming to live down here, I wanted to kill both of you.'

'You—you knew he phoned me? I mean, how did you——'

'I listened. That day in the office. I was standing right behind my door.'

'Oh, *no!*' She was horrified. 'I had no idea! I thought—I thought——'

'You thought I was working at my desk, that there was no chance of your being overheard. Well, I didn't overhear, I eavesdropped. I was just about to come out of my office when I heard your exclamation of delight, *Garry!* You'll never know how I felt in that instant.'

'Delight? Oh, Blake, it wasn't delight! It was amazement. I was dumbfounded.'

He shook his head ruefully. 'Given that I believed

you were in love with the man, to my ears it was delight. I was convinced you were taking up with him again. When I spotted you in town that time, when I was in the restaurant and you looked straight at me and then vanished, it seemed to be all the confirmation I needed. You didn't even want to say hello to me for old times' sake. You cut me dead. Can you imagine how I felt?'

Ruth groaned. 'Yes. Yes, believe me, I know. You weren't even supposed to know about Garry, about that meeting . . .'

'I'm well aware of that. That's why I called you into my office. It was to give you the chance to tell me you were going to meet him. I'd heard every word you said, Ruth. I got you into my office and I deliberately asked you what had been happening in yours. I asked you about messages and phone calls you'd taken. And you sat there, smiling at me innocently. I wanted to throttle you. If nothing else, I thought you liked me and trusted me enough to tell me of such an important meeting. I couldn't tell you how I was feeling, that I was as jealous as hell, not without making an ass of myself, embarrassing you. Instead, I told you to go. I couldn't bear to be with you, even to see you, any longer. Right then I almost hated you, God forgive me. But there you were, looking at me with that butter-wouldn't-melt expression, those big brown eyes of yours smiling at me.

'I thought you deceitful, I was hurt, besides everything else, that you wouldn't confide in me. Of course I know now how wrong I was. I know why you went to meet Garry, Wendy's told me all about it. And I want to say now, I think it was big of you, the way you handled him. It was generous of you. It convinces me he's well and truly out of your system, otherwise you couldn't have done what you did.'

'Oh, Blake, Blake! Garry was out of my system a long time ago. I was in love with love, not him. Somewhere along the line, perhaps from social pressures, the pattern of things in my own family, I'd thought it was time to marry. I'd only known Garry a few months before he went to Saudi. I got engaged to him after knowing him for three weeks. And it wasn't as though I'd spent all that much time with him, what with him sometimes working night-shifts and me working in the day and—oh, I don't know! It was a mistake,' she added lamely, wearily. 'I suppose he was that bit different from the other men I'd been out with, different enough to fascinate me for a while, to make me think I was in love with him.'

'But why didn't you tell me?' Blake persisted. 'Why?'

'Self-preservation.'

'*What?*'

She sighed. 'I—thought that as long as you believed I loved Garry, you'd never suspect how I felt about you.'

'You were right.' He looked grim. 'Dead right.'

'And, well . . .' She looked away, a little embarrassed.

'And? And what? Go *on.*'

He was right. She had to tell him everything. 'And it also helped protect me from you, from your advances.'

He almost smiled. 'It did?'

'To some extent. It helped to keep you in line. It stopped things from going too far.'

Blake slipped an arm around her shoulders. 'And what would have been so awful about that? You wanted me as much as I wanted you.' He laughed. 'Why am I still using the past tense?'

Ruth didn't laugh, she couldn't. 'I didn't want to

have an affair with you. I didn't want to be just a number on your list of conquests. One of many.'

Almost sadly, lamenting all their lost time, he said, 'I never wanted an affair with you, Ruth. In my male arrogance, I believed I could make you forget Garry. I believed that, and I hoped—hoped—that in time you would come to love me. But I didn't want to seduce you, I knew there'd be no point in doing that, which is is why I always accepted the situation when you called a halt. I didn't want to seduce you only to have you resent me afterwards.'

'I see.' Her eyes were twinkling. 'You were right when you referred to your male arrogance. You think you could have won me over on the physical level, do you?'

'Don't you?' His eyes were twinkling, too.

'Yes!'

They laughed. They laughed a little too loudly, a little too long. Next to crying, it was the best means of giving vent to all sorts of emotions. Tears were inappropriate now, uncalled for, but in both of them there was still a residue of tension, a certain weariness from all they'd been through.

And then in the midst of their laughter, they were kissing again. 'You see,' he teased, 'I'm not awesome, after all. I can't imagine why you felt you couldn't be honest with me about how you felt. I had good reasons for holding back, you didn't.'

'Oh!' Ruth protested but she did so lightly, airily. 'Now who's being unfair? What about that blonde I met in your house that night? I mean, it wasn't just that, it was—well, your attitude towards the women in your life, the way they came and went. You never made any bones about it, and of course I admired your openness but . . .' Her tone changed radically. 'But, Blake, it was knowing the end was in sight that frightened me so much. Knowing you were going to leave the country for good at some point next—this— year. Worse, you never told me about it. You only told me half your dream. You never confided wholly in me, and I thought I knew why not.'

He was looking at her with a mixture of astonishment and puzzlement. 'What are you talking about? Greece? My retiring? Who told you about that?'

'Not you. Do you see?'

'Of course I see.' Suddenly he was on his feet, too frustrated to remain seated. 'Ruth, that particular plan was abandoned within a week of my meeting you! There's no way I'm going to live permanently in Greece! There's no way I'd send my children to school overseas. Heaven help me, what kind of crazy world is this? How can two people—who told you about all that stuff?'

'Dinah.'

'Dinah!' It was as if he couldn't believe it. 'What does she know about it? I mean, what does she know about what goes on in my head?'

'Don't be daft, Blake! It's been an obsession of yours for years and years!'

'Yes, but—good *grief*! Not for the past six months, it hasn't. Not since I fell for *you*. Dinah! How could she? She had no right to interfere! How dare she! When did——' He stopped abruptly. He sank into an armchair, appearing suddenly as if all the weight of the world were on his shoulders. 'Now I *am* being unfair.'

'Yes, you are,' Ruth said gently. 'Dinah mentioned it to me some time ago, the day I passed my driving test, to be precise. As a matter of fact, she was warning me against falling in love with you. And she was right to, so you needn't look indignant! Anyhow, I told her with absolute conviction she needn't worry about me.

She believed me. She was bound to, I think I believed it at the time. Well, almost! Oh, Blake, it seems to me we could all do with a lesson in mind-reading. How could Dinah know you'd changed your mind, your plans, your *dream*, if you never told her?'

'She couldn't,' he agreed. 'And I never did tell her.'

'You never told me, either.'

'Why should I have? I wasn't aware you knew my plans for retirement in the first place! It never occurred to me to *un*inform you!'

'You see what I mean about the mind-reading lessons? Dinah and I—I mean, you went and bought a house in Greece! It all seemed to be nearing fruition.'

He was nodding in agreement. 'I'd wanted that house for years. I knew the people who owned it, they'd promised to give me first refusal if they ever wanted to sell. It's gorgeous, Ruth, perfect for holidays.' He forgot himself, searching his pockets till he found a photograph.

Ruth watched him, her eyes shining with love for him. When he held out the photo, she went over to him and planted herself on his knee. She saw a small white house on a hillside; the picture must have been taken from a boat because in the foreground there was the twinkling sea and in the background, a brilliant, deep blue sky. A cloudless sky. 'It's very pretty, Blake.'

'Yes. You'll love it, I promise you. It isn't big but it's certainly pretty. And it has no telephone,' he added enthusiastically, as if this were one of its best amenities. 'It's on a tiny island where the mail gets delivered only twice a week. In other words,' he smiled, his arms closing tightly around her, 'it's also perfect for a honeymoon. That stretch of beach there is ours. Strictly private.'

Ruth handed the photo back to him. 'You were

there two weeks. Did you have last minute doubts about buying it?'

'No, no. It was you who kept me away for so long.'

'Me? I couldn't wait for you to come back. I . . . yes, quite so. Ah, well.'

'I used the house-purchase as an excuse to stay in Greece. In fact, I needed time to think. Time when I wouldn't have you around as a distraction. I didn't know whether to fire you at that point or whether to take a shot in the dark and ask you to marry me.'

She shook him. 'Idiot! If you'd made a proper proposal, you might have changed the whole course of our history! As it was, it seemed like the most ridiculous thing I'd ever heard you come out with.'

'Darling, what else could I do? I was far too afraid, too proud to put my heart on the table, inviting a bashing and humiliation. In any case,' he added, grinning. 'I'm not one for flowery language, my sweet, darling, precious, brown-eyed beauty.'

Ruth laughed. And laughed. How right he was! It didn't suit him, not a bit. 'It was a fair attempt, Blake, but I'd rather you put it more simply. Do you think you could manage to tell me in three words how you feel about me?'

'I——'

The telephone rang.

Foolishly, quite without thinking they both swivelled their heads to look at the instrument as though it were an unwelcome stranger who'd walked into the room.

'Shall I let it ring?'

'Yes. No. Better not. Tell them you'll call back, that it's inconvenient right now because you're just being proposed to and the poor fellow is down on one knee and . . .'

Giggling, Ruth had picked up the receiver before

he'd finished. 'Wendy! Hi!' She was surprised, Wendy was the last person she'd expected to ring. 'Oh!' Being told very firmly to listen, just listen, Ruth did so. 'Oh! ... *Oh*! Wendy! We'll be right over. Don't do anything. I mean, don't ... just hold on. *Don't panic!* We're coming straight away.'

She plonked the receiver down, turning to find Blake already on his feet. 'What's up? What is it?'

'The baby! It's coming!'

'The baby? But she told me today it wasn't due for five weeks.'

'It's early!'

'How marvellous! Come on then, let's get over there if she needs us.'

'Marvellous?' Ruth was positively twitching. 'Oh, I don't know, I don't know about that! Blake, Derek isn't home yet. We must get there quickly, give her support.'

'Now hold on. Calm down.' He put both hands on the top of her shoulders. 'Where is Derek? Why isn't he home?'

'She's packing her case for the hospital. Oh! He—I don't know, he's at some meeting or other. In London. He should be back any minute, Wendy said, but——'

'Okay, okay. How often are the pains coming?'

'What?' She looked at him blankly. What did he know about such things? More than she, evidently. 'I don't know, I didn't think to ask! Oh, wait a minute, wait a minute, she said—she said something about every twenty minutes——'

Blake relaxed visibly. 'Oh, well, that's all right. There's no need to panic, lady. Plenty of time for you to comb your hair, put on your coat. It's freezing out there.'

Ruth dashed to the hall. Comb her hair, indeed!

What the devil did he know? No cause for panic? Every twenty minutes . . . and he was talking about the *weather*!

By the time they got to the house, Derek was home. Home and white with worry. He was panicking. Wendy was, too, though hers didn't show so much.

There was a chorus of 'Oh, am I glad to see you!'

'Derek's been home for about ninety seconds,' Wendy added. 'He's just put my case in the car. We're off.'

Ruth looked from her future husband to her brother. 'Would you like Blake to drive you?'

'I would rather.' Derek looked apologetically at Blake. 'Is that okay with you? Honestly, I planned *not* to feel like this. But it's coming five weeks early . . . Wendy's always said it would be early.'

'He,' Wendy amended.

'She's always said it'll be a boy, too.'

All this was news to Ruth.

'And it's going to be all right,' Wendy put in. 'That's something else I'm sure of now. So I don't want any of you worrying about me.'

'We'll worry all we like,' Blake told her with a smile. 'Come on, folks. Let's get to the hospital.'

They went in Derek's car and Blake drove carefully, sensibly and in no particular hurry. Nobody spoke on the journey, there was nothing but the sound of the engine and Wendy's occasional gasps. When that happened, Ruth grabbed hold of Blake's thigh while Derek, on the back seat with his wife, said 'Oh! *Oh*!'

Wendy was whisked away at the hospital. Derek, his sister and Blake were ushered by a nurse into a waiting room.

'But I'm going with my wife!' Derek protested. 'I'm going to *be* there!'

The nurse beamed at him. 'Of *course* you are, Mr

Boyd. But not just yet! I'll come for you in plenty of time, don't you worry about that.'

For what seemed an eternity they sat, the three of them, in a state of excited expectation. Ruth was in between the two men. On one side of her was Blake, holding her hand tightly, giving her reassurance. On the other was Derek, whose hand she was holding tightly, giving him reassurance.

'It occurs to me,' Blake said at length, so matter-of-factly it was in itself comical, 'that we look like the three monkeys. I wish someone were here to take a photo, it'd certainly give Wendy a laugh when she saw it.'

It was some time later that Derek started the floor-pacing routine. Ruth and Blake grinned at each other, whispering, 'I wondered when that would happen!'

'He hung on a long time, didn't he?'

'I don't know why I'm being so cocky,' Blake confessed, 'I dread to think what I'll be like when it's you they've got in there!'

'You'll be like this, mate!' Derek surprised them. He'd heard every word. Then, his brow clearing, he stared at them suddenly. It was as though he'd only just realised who they were. 'What are you two doing here? I mean, *together*. I mean, what's——'

'Mr Boyd, you may come through now.' The nurse was back, a big, reassuring smile on her face.

For just a second, Derek seemed rooted to the spot. With a quick, unseeing look at his supporters, he strode after the retreating nurse.

'That's pretty quick,' said Blake.

'Are you some kind of authority?'

He started tickling her. 'Blake, stop that! Have a little respect for your surroundings!'

He stopped it at once. He kissed her instead.

Fortunately, he wasn't kissing her later, much later,

when Derek came back. It was five minutes to four. In the morning.

'I have a son,' Derek said simply, his face wreathed in smiles. '*I have a son!* They're fine, both of them. It was as easy as anything!'

Ruth was laughing her head off, joyous. Lord, what a day, what a day this had been! She would never, ever, forget one single minute of it.

'Tell that to Wendy in the morning!' Blake shook Derek's hand. 'Congratulations, Pop!'

Ruth kissed her brother. 'Congratulations! Oh, Derek! How marvellous! Will they throw us all out now, or can we take a peek at him?'

'I daresay that could be arranged.'

With Derek seeming to grow several inches before their eyes, Ruth and Blake followed him out of the waiting-room.

'Aren't you coming in?'

Blake slowed his car to a halt outside Pine Court. Dawn was breaking. They had taken Derek home and shared a bottle of champagne with him. He'd been asleep on the sofa before they'd got out of his living-room. Ruth had covered him with the duvet from the bed and said a prayer of thanks—not her first that night—for the tremendous wealth she had been blessed with in her family, all of them, especially its tiny, healthy, beautiful new addition.

She looked at Blake now. Another addition. No, she was an addition to his. Soon, she would be Mrs Blake Marsden and they, the couple, would be a family in their own right.

He laughed at her. 'Of course I'm coming in. Try and stop me. But just for a little while,' he added pointedly.

'Humm, I think that should have been my line.

Gosh, I could use a cup of coffee!'

'You and me both. And I think Derek's going to need a week in bed!'

'Oh, he'll be fine tomorrow. I know him. He'll rally now his panic's over. Now the baby's safe. His son,' she added softly, smiling.

Blake caught hold of her, his hand reaching to brush gently against her cheek. 'I'm glad you feel that way about children, darling. I—I'm ...' He stopped, unable to go on.

Seeing a curious brightness in his eyes, Ruth took his hand and held it tightly in both her own, her heart almost bursting with love for him.

It was almost half an hour later before she discovered what he was going to say. It was when she asked him, 'So what are we going to do? When we're married? What are your plans now? Our plans. What of your *dream*, Blake?'

She put a second cup of coffee on the table beside him. He pulled her on to his knee. 'Now, I have one dream only. And it's going to last a lifetime! It'll start with a long, long, long honeymoon.'

'I approve.'

'Don't you want to know how long?'

She nodded.

'Say six months?' He was perfectly serious.

'I approve.'

'Thereafter I shall work but it won't quite be business as usual. I'm going to delegate more to Dinah and Rory, especially Rory. He can take over all the sales, travelling included. He's up to it. Neither of them is working to their full potential, which is my fault, I suppose. I'll just keep a part-time eye on things.' He sought her comment with his eyes, his arms closing tightly around her.

'I approve.'

His eyebrows went up. 'No argument at all, eh? That's how I like my women to be, compliant! And you won't be working at all. Except in the house, and then only if you want to. How does that grab you?'

'I approve.'

He grinned. 'And in the course of time, after we've seen something of the world together, I hope we'll have children of our own. Well?'

'I approve.'

He was laughing at her now. 'Is that all you can say? Now listen, lady, I'm going to leave you in five minutes. We've got to get some sleep. Hmm ... However, during the next five minutes, I'm going to kiss you good night. Now what do you say to *that*?'

She smiled.

Harlequin Presents

Coming Next Month

927 AN ELUSIVE MISTRESS Lindsay Armstrong
An interior designer from Brisbane finally finds a man to share the rest of her life with—only to have her ex-husband return and reawaken feelings she'd thought were hidden forever.

928 ABODE OF PRINCES Jayne Bauling
In mysterious Rajasthan, Fate prompts a young woman to redefine her understanding of love and friendship. But the man she meets and loves will hear nothing of her breaking her engagement for him.

929 POPPY GIRL Jaqueline Gilbert
Dreams of wealth don't overwhelm a prospective heiress. But a certain Frenchman does. If only she didn't come to suspect his motives for sweeping her off her feet.

930 LOVE IS A DISTANT SHORE Claire Harrison
A reporter with a knack for getting to the heart of the matter disturbs the concentration of a young woman planning to swim Lake Ontario. Surely she should concentrate on one goal at a time.

931 CAPABLE OF FEELING Penny Jordan
In sharing a roof to help care for her boss's niece and nephew, a young woman comes to terms with her inability to express love. Is it too late to change the confines of their marriage agreement?

932 VILLA IN THE SUN Marjorie Lewty
Villa Favorita is the private paradise she shared with her husband—until his fortunes plummeted and he drove her away. Now she has been asked to handle the sale. Little does she know how closely her husband follows the market.

933 LAND OF THUNDER Annabel Murray
The past is a blank to this accident victim. She feels a stranger to her "husband." Worse, their new employer touches something disturbing within her. Something's terribly wrong here.

934 THE FINAL PRICE Patricia Wilson
In Illyaros, where her Greek grandfather lies ill, her ex-husband denies both their divorce and her right to remarry. Yet he was unfaithful to her! No wonder she hasn't told him about the birth of their son.

Available in November wherever paperback books are sold, or through Harlequin Reader Service:

In the U.S.
P.O. Box 1397
Buffalo, N.Y.
14240-1397

In Canada
P.O. Box 2800, Postal Station A
5170 Yonge Street
Willowdale, Ontario M2N 6J3

ATTRACTIVE, SPACE SAVING BOOK RACK

Display your most prized novels on this handsome and sturdy book rack. The hand-rubbed walnut finish will blend into your library decor with quiet elegance, providing a practical organizer for your favorite hard-or soft-covered books.

Only $9.95

Approximately 16" x 8" when assembled

Assembles in seconds!

To order, rush your name, address and zip code, along with a check or money order for $10.70 ($9.95 plus 75¢ postage and handling) (New York residents add appropriate sales tax), payable to *Harlequin Reader Service* to:

In the U.S.

Harlequin Reader Service
Book Rack Offer
901 Fuhrmann Blvd.
P.O. Box 1325
Buffalo, NY 14269-1325

Offer not available in Canada.

Take
4 novels
and a
surprise gift
FREE

HARLEQUIN HISTORICAL

Explore love with Harlequin in the Middle Ages, the Renaissance, in the Regency, the Victorian and other eras.

Relive within these books the endless ages of romance, set against authentic historical backgrounds. Two new historical love stories published each month.